STRANGE BATTLEFIELDS

Four Queens

BY
JERRY ADAMS

STRANGE BATTLEFIELDS

Copyrights ©2025 JERRY ADAMS

All rights reserved.

No part of this book may be reproduced, stored in a retrieval system, or transmitted in any form or by any means—electronic, mechanical, photocopying, recording, or otherwise—without the prior written permission of the author, except in the case of brief quotations embodied in critical articles or reviews.

Table of Contents

PROLOGUE v
Chapter 1 1
Chapter 2 11
Chapter 3 20
Chapter 4 26
Chapter 5 33
Chapter 6 36
Chapter 7 41
Chapter 8 49
Chapter 9 57
Chapter 10 60
Chapter 11 72
Chapter 12 80
Chapter 13 84
Chapter 14 93
Chapter 15 101
Chapter 16 106
Chapter 17 113
Chapter 18 119
Chapter 19 126
Chapter 20 131
Chapter 21 137
Chapter 22 145

Chapter 23 152

Chapter 24 172

Chapter 25 175

Chapter 26 181

Chapter 27 186

PROLOGUE

STRANGE BATTLEFIELDS

On the face of Mt. Ozark, Tony Gianni had bronzed in a placard

All wars are fought twice,

The first time on the battlefield,

The second time in memory………

Memory is haunted, not just by ghostly others but by the horrors we
have done, seen, and condoned, or by The unspeakable things from which we have profited

***

Veterans for peace

STRANGE BATTLEFIELDS

Chapter 1

Traffic was flowing nicely for a Friday morning in the "Big Apple." It was springtime, so there was a vision of pigeons making their way to the fresh emerald-green grass growing in Central Park for new earthworms. Tony Gianni's yellow cab taxi was taking him to LaGuardia for his Southern Airways flight south to Birmingham, Alabama.

As he looked out the backseat window, reflections reminded him of the last time he flew south, but then it was to Biloxi, Mississippi, to renew his stature as "Boss" over the gambling syndicate. This time, however, it was a debt overdue for thirty years.

As the son of a capo from the DiRaggo family, he'd been sent South to hide out and learn how to blend with a "crew," also known as the "Dixie Mafia."

After finding his seat for the flight, which would have a layover in Atlanta, he went back into his reverie as to why he was going to this particular destination.

They arrived in Vietnam after a brief training period in Korea. Both men were drafted, and after advanced infantry training at Fort Benning, including jump school, it was time to proceed as soldiers to be accounted for. He arrived in Vietnam on the same troop carrier as Hershel McCoy from Tuscaloosa, Alabama.

They had become best friends in a short period, and as luck would have it, they traveled from Korea together on the "rickety" old ship that transported troops all over the Far East. During their passage, each told of how they had arrived at this point, and each tried to find a common denominator in their swift approach to a binding relationship.

Soldiers from far too many wars had relationships with "buddies" in their units that lasted many years. Those relationships, as this one was, definitely could not be described as consanguineous, but at times, you felt, as a rule, via their storied descriptions, like you were kin. Later, this was what he told Bea, the widow of his deceased friend, Hershel.

The plane arrived in Atlanta on time, but the Captain announced there would be an extra hour layover due to a procedure the airline described as a "minor inspection." Therefore, the passengers could leave the plane to get lunch but were advised to listen for the announcement that the flight to Birmingham would leave in fifteen to thirty minutes.

He got off to stretch his legs and grab a sandwich at a kiosk, but with all of that activity, his eyes, awareness, and memories could only see the many servicemen congregated at various points throughout the terminal. It took him back thirty years when he, too, was here to catch a flight to Ft. Lewis, Washington, for assignment to the FarEast.

Little did he know, in just a few hours, thru his memory, he'd go back there.

As he sat in the third row, number four seat, a young soldier sat down next to him, wearing the arm patch of the 7thCalvary. Since he was a veteran, he observed that the soldier had been serving in combat and wounded, as his chest ribbons carried the Purple Heart medal. Tony also noticed he was a Buck Sergeant. The young man said nothing and didn't even acknowledge Tony's existence. Never mind, thought Tony, "Kid probably has a lot on his mind."

After they became airborne, the stewardess came by to get drink orders. As she approached them, Tony spoke first and said, "Give me a bourbon and Seven-Up, and this young lad, if he is old enough, whatever he wants."

The young man quickly turned to Tony and said, "Thanks, sir, but I shall refrain from alcohol. But may I have a Coke instead?"

Tony and the stewardess nodded their heads—yes.

The soldier twisted his body to get a better look at Tony and said, "Bet you are a veteran, sir, and thanks for the offer of a drink. Normally, I'd take you up on this, but I'm in training for my upcoming assignment."

Tony answered with a smile, "Yep. In Nam with the 25th Combat Engineers."

"What'cha do now?" asked the young soldier.

"Pretty much nothing, but guess you must say I'm a professional gambler."

Both men laughed at this response.

"Where will you be when you arrive at your destination?" asked the soldier.

"In Biloxi. That's my hometown now. Born and grew up in the Bronx of New York City. Gotta important appointment in Tuscaloosa," said Tony.

"Well, not sure how long I'll be assigned at Fort Benning, but feel like I'll be sent back overseas," said the young man.

The drinks were served and consumed just as the announcement was made that landing would be shortly and to buckleup.

As they were shuffling out the door in Birmingham, the young man introduced himself as Keith Brewer Jr. from Florence, Alabama.

After collecting his baggage, Tony went to the Hertz kiosk and rented the Ford he'd use on this visit, plus he would drive on afterward to Biloxi after his meeting.

He drove out of town on the freeway for a while and exited to take Highway 82 west toward Tuscaloosa. At the diner where he stopped to get a meal, he met some students from Bama who were hyper over the latest win against Mississippi State. Since he'd become a resident of Mississippi, he'd embraced Ole Miss as "his school," so he didn't care, but he was glad to see young people having fun.

After he began the last leg of his journey, he thought that since he'd lived in the South so long, his being, speech, dress, and occupation were now all Southern. Saying "y'all" was common now. In the Bronx, every person he met commented on this. Actually, now his true occupation was tied to a casino, but he lived in a house in Pascagoula on a fashionable houseboat. He also had a room in the Golden Nugget, where he worked on occasion.

It had been thirty years since he'd worn an Army uniform, but meeting the young Sergeant, brought him back to those days of fearing for his life and having no one to care for him. All of this further brought him back to the memory of his Army "buddy," Hershel McCoy. Actually, his memory was why he was driving to the home of the University of Alabama. He was to meet with Hershel's widow, Bea, and their son, Bobby, to tell them what happened that caused Hershel's death almost thirty years ago. This was his own request to finally tell them the true facts. A phone call was made two weeks ago to her, and after explaining who he was, she agreed to meet with him, provided her son, Bobby, was allowed to attend and hear what he had to say. Strangely, when he began his quest to find her, there wasn't a problem in doing so. She had never remarried and still used the last name McCoy. When he asked the telephone operator for information, her number was easy to find. At first, she thought it was some type of cruel joke, but as Tony began identifying himself, she realized this was a wish come true for her son and this lonely widow. They made arrangements to meet at the First Methodist in Northport, which wasn't too far from the Ramada

Inn where he'd checked in. Part of the plan was to meet near noon and then go to "Dreamland" for lunch. He told her Hershel had spoken many times about this café, and he wanted to eat there. She laughed about his request and agreed to do it, provided her son could attend. Tony relinquished his wish to meet with her alone and said yes, of course.

That evening, he just drove around town to browse the fame the football program had brought to this rural area. He found "Dreamland" but refrained from eating there tonight, though the aroma was very tempting. He settled at a Waffle House for a plate of Ham and eggs.

After settling in his room, he felt anxiety about meeting Hershel's wife and son and, naturally, how and what he'd say, but he dismissed the thought of not sleeping and dropped off without knowledge.

In the morning, he dressed in his jogging suit and drove to the mall to exercise heartily via speed walking. He did this for an hour and then returned to his motel room, took a shower, and went for breakfast at the same Waffle House, reading the newspaper to help kill time before he met with Hershel's family.

He dressed in a dark grey suit with shined shoes but no tie. The light blue shirt, unbuttoned, was enough. He followed the desk clerk's directions and found the church as described. An ancient Plymouth was parked near the front door, carrying a lady and a young man. He got out and walked toward the door when the two occupants opened their doors and stood up for him to see. A lady's voice asked, "Are you Tony Gianni?"

"Yes, I am," Tony replied.

The three met at the rear of the ancient vehicle and shook hands. Tony, in sizing them up, later remarked, "They looked like movie stars, actually. He just wasn't prepared for their image. She was like

Doris Day, and he like James Dean." He was glad he wore a suit, but he felt "shaggy" compared to them. Both gave him brilliant smiles and locked eyes with him, showing nothing but friendliness.

Bea spoke first. "Tony, I'm so glad to meet you. You look how Hershel described you in his letters."

Bobby then said, "Sir, this is a real blessing for Mom and me. Your phone call was a prayer answered for us."

"Sorry, I had no way of knowing how you would look, but I am very glad to meet both of you," said Tony.

Bea then said, "You mentioned Dreamland. Do you still want to go there?"

"Yeah. Do y'all want to ride with me and show me the way?" said Tony.

"Before we leave, I want it understood that we're treating you to this meal, and please don't try to do the masculine thing and insist on paying. We know you've gone out of your way to do this, and we are grateful and flattered, okay?" announced Bea.

"Very well, shall we go?" said Tony.

Both answered yes and entered Tony's car, with Bea in the backseat and Bobby riding "shotgun" and talking to Tony constantly. In that conversation, he learned Bobby was a senior at Bama majoring in business, and Bea was a secretary at the church where he'd met them. In addition, she remarked that she'd never married again but was now engaged to a fellow church member named Daniel, who was an attorney.

At the fabled "Dreamland," Tony was taken aback by the cuisine and building. They ate outside at a long table with newspapers spread out covering the homemade wooden surface. Steel chairs, one large roll of paper towels strategically placed in the middle, and condiments of many descriptions made up the setting.

An iced-down pitcher of sweet iced tea and very few utensils completed the eating area. Tony ordered a plank of ribs and one pulled pork sandwich. Later on, he got a bowl of Mike Adams' infamous banana pudding. The couple ate a barbecue plate. Lunch took an hour, and Tony was "stuffed," but Hershel had bragged about this place the whole time he'd known him, and now he understood why.

During lunch, the couple decided this wasn't the place to hear what Tony had to say and recommended they return to the church and use one of the meeting rooms for privacy.

They returned to the church just as a thunderstorm burst open.

A friendship was growing, even as raindrops fell on their anointed heads by an angel passing by.

Could it be Hershel?

Inside, the facial expressions on the couple had become more somber, though. It was time for Hershel to begin:

"We met on a troop carrier sailing us from Korea to Vietnam. We had to bunk side by side in the bowels of the U.S.S. General Mann. Both of us experienced morbid seasickness. But thanks to a medic and the ship's store selling Hi-C lime drinks and Cheez-Its, we survived. Normal food just made matters worse. Some muffins and coffee for breakfast were some help, but ol' Hershel barfed that up too.

We got off and reported to a repo depot and learned we'd both been assigned to the 25th Combat Engineers with a MOS of combat soldier.

We began work as trainees learning how to survey roads, trails, and airstrips. All we did at first, though, was extend measuring tapes, but in time, we learned how to use the instruments. On our third mission of construction, Hershel was shot for the first time. We were building a road going into the jungle. We had cleared most of the terrain, and I took the right side of the road while Hershel took the left."

We were spreading the tape when a V.C. sniper began pelting us. We both dove to the ground instead of being targets, and Tony's right boot caught a clump of rock as he fell, leaving the entire boot still exposed. Tony didn't know this, y'all, and after a couple of shots went over our bodies, one round in the fourth volley hit Hershel's Achilles' heel, and I heard him moan. I asked if he was all right. His answer was, "I'm hit, Tony. Tony, I'm hit, help me."

I crawled across the road and saw his face. He was hurting, so I got on the walkie-talkie and yelled, "MEDIC!" and started dragging him toward me with the intent of getting both of us out of harm's way by going under a parked vehicle. But before we got this done, two medics in a jeep jumped out and began administering first aid, plus a shot for pain. I was just prone in the dirt and moved my body around to be in a position to fire back at the V.C. sniper. As soon as I was properly in place, I began to fire back at the gook—I mean, rapid firing. I don't know if I hit him, but we were able to stop the bleeding in his ankle and load him up for further medical care. The jeep took him to a plateau where, later, a helicopter picked him up and flew him to a Naval Hospital Ship where they saved his life.

I didn't know anything else about him for over a month. In the meantime, he got his heel repaired, and physical therapy got him back to walking again. To this day, I don't understand why they didn't send him home. He really wasn't needed where I was, but one Monday morning, I looked up, and there he was, hobbling toward me with that ol' cheesy grin, saying, "How ya doin', Yankee boy?"

We shook hands, and I went to the OIC and got him assigned to our group. We were in the jungle now, building assignment camps for platoons to get relief from the long sieges we were enduring. I had topped out as a surveyor, and this was my assignment. Tony wanted to use the transit when we had to do a certain angle.

You know, now I remember what he actually said on that day and our dialogue about the mission problem. I told him to record all he'd done because I had to return to home base to replenish our food and water, plus pick up the mail. I distinctly told him not to get out in the open. The V.C. was near. I told him to cut an opening in the banana tree leaf to place the transit at an angle to see. Actually, it wasn't the safest thing to do, but he was bent and determined to do this. And he complied—until I departed.

I was told later that he told Higgins, our metric man, he just couldn't see and moved out in the open. As he was making an adjustment, a V.C. sniper shot him between the eyes. He never knew anything about what had happened. He died instantly.

He stopped talking, looking deep into Bea's blue eyes and seeing such anguish. Plus, Bobby had dropped his head and was staring at the floor. In addition, reliving the pains and fears of war was taking a toll on him.

He stepped over to a window and was looking out when Bea asked, "What happened to you during this time?"

"Shortly after I returned and got out of the jeep, Higgins told me what happened and showed me his body under a blanket. I took a look to make sure it was him, and it was. We began to set up for a skirmish with the V.C., but they didn't wait on us and came toward us, firing wide open. We lost two other men, and I was hit in the shoulder, but all of us in this group were firing back and were successful in stopping the attack by killing several of them.

"I had to have a blood transfusion and was taken back to HQ hospital, where I was cared for nicely. I spent two weeks in the hospital, recovered, and was reassigned to light duty. Just as I became a short-timer, I got reassigned."

Bea stood, walked over to Tony, embraced him, and said, "Tony, it took a lot of courage for you to do this, and you'll never know how much Bobby and I appreciate what you've done and said. You are a true friend of Hershel's and now of Bobby and me. Please come back and visit anytime."

They all walked out together, shook hands again, and Bea went to find Daniel, Bobby to Bama, and Tony to Biloxi.

Chapter 2

Tony drove straight to Biloxi and arrived that evening, tired and hungry. He went to the Hertz office and cleared his turn-in with a young night clerk, called a taxi, and about an hour later was opening the door to his fashionable houseboat. After taking care of his luggage and its contents, he sat down at his desk and phoned Gail, his manager at the bookstore and, for the last year, the woman he cared for—now to the point of almost calling it love.

"Hi, Gail. How is it going?"

"Missing you. Are you home yet?"

"Yes, just got here. Gonna have a snack and crash—I'm bushed."

"Imagine so. Did you get the deed finished?"

"Yeah, will tell you about it tomorrow. Wanna have dinner at the club?"

"Sounds great. Okay, meet me there around six o'clock, and if possible, could you come back here with me? I need your company, and I feel there are some things I need to talk to you about. Would that be okay?" he asked.

"Right now, I say yes to all you asked from me, but, you know, I must make sure I have people available, okay," said Gail.

"Sure, honey."

"Tony, you've never called me that."

"My fault, will start doing better."

"Just tell me this—what did she look like?"

"Doris Day, but engaged."

"Wow, you got all the story, I bet."

"No, Gail, this was my best friend's wife. I had no such ideas."

She just laughed and said goodbye.

Tony slept for the remainder of the day, and when he arose, he felt as if a load had been lifted from his shoulders. He prepared an omelet for breakfast, went for a quick swim, and again felt rejuvenated enough to do some minor repairs on his home, plus he gave it a good cleaning inside. Before he knew it, the time to get "gussied up" was here, and he wanted to look "slick" tonight. So, quickly, he got himself ready and left for the country club to meet Gail.

He'd worked himself into his second food craving, and for this evening, he thought about prime beef or a T-bone. He arrived on time, and as always, she would be late, so he went to the bar for his customary bourbon and Seven-Up. He drank slowly but was on his second drink when she entered the bar to get him. Tonight, he had to take a second look at her to recognize her. She was extremely put together, wearing a sleek new dress—tight, sexy, and black. Perfect accessories, pumps, and her hair, very stylish. He got out of his chair and, without taking his eyes off her beautiful chocolate ones, went directly to her and kissed those luscious red lips.

"Stop, sir, I hardly know you," she said kiddingly.

"Gail, you are magnificent tonight. You probably did miss me."

"Told you so," she said as they made their way to their table.

"By the way," she said, "you don't look so bad yourself—like Dean Martin."

They went back to the houseboat, nicknamed *Non Gratum Anus Rodentum*, to conclude their evening. He left his Lincoln at the club and rode with her. She had no alcohol that evening, and he had two more cocktails, which, in an arrest, would get him busted for being under the influence. She would take him back tomorrow to retrieve it, but that evening was all about romance—to start with—but she was in for another surprise: a different side of the man she was now having love thoughts about.

Upon arrival, he opened a bottle of wine for her and fixed another cocktail. He had his back to her when she asked, "Tell me, sir, what are your intentions tonight?"

He turned and looked into her eyes as he said, "Gail, I would like very much to make our relationship closer. I've become more attracted to you, but first, we must really get to know each other better. Do you believe any relationship can grow without trust?"

"Yes, but how are we to establish trust between the two of us?"

"Tell each other truthfully *all* about ourselves. If you agree, sit back and listen to my true story."

She kicked her shoes off and sat back on the sofa as he began:

"I was born and raised in New York City. My father was a member of a mafia family, and my mother was the daughter of the *capo* of Newark, New Jersey—the kind of people you'd never know. My existing family owned a record shop and studio in Queens and knew a lot of famous entertainers. They were big members of Saint Peter's and attended mass each Sunday. At one time in my life, I was an altar boy.

When I became a teenager, I noticed a cute little girl at church named Annette Rico. She was attracted to me too. We went on all the typical teen dates, but on one rainy afternoon, we found ourselves alone in her house, and after a lot of kissing, we tried sex. Time passed quickly. Two months later, she told me she hadn't had her period and was afraid of being pregnant. I told her to wait another month, and if it didn't start, we'd tell her parents. However, her mother was more astute about incidences involving her daughter and quizzed her about our relationship. She broke down and confessed everything.

That evening, when my father came home, he began to shout at me and slap me around. It seems her father called mine and told him there was no way she would have an abortion—I must marry her. My father agreed, and we got married in a small town north of the city, with only our parents attending. She remained at her home, and I at mine.

I was beginning to get somewhat happy over knocking this girl up, but she had a miscarriage, and I thought this would be the end of it all. I entered Fordham that fall and lived on campus. But one evening, two men followed me from class to my room, and when I went out to socialize with my friends, they got closer to me. On the second night, they finally approached me and said, 'You will not get away with knocking Annette up.'

I went home then and told my parents what had happened, and I saw the fear on my father's face. He went to the basement for a long time, but when he came back up, he had made a plan. That changed my life. I was sent here in an eighteen-wheeler truck and met with Jeff Adamo, who put me up in an apartment above the old Ocean Spa Casino. I worked there as a card dealer and bouncer. The pay was fair, and the food was great. Jeff was my teacher and friend, which I guess could be known as my mentor.

During this time, I was the only daytime dealer at the blackjack table, and many women came in to gamble—mostly Air Force wives and girlfriends and a few regulars from town. On one occasion, I met the Commanding General of the Air Force Base's wife. She was addicted to many things—mostly gambling and sex.

I talked to Jeff about her, and he advised me not to take her to bed and to allow her to win occasionally in order to keep her coming back with other women gamblers. I understood the General knew about her but looked the other way and indulged in his own vices. What they were, I never found out."

I began to notice more females coming around, so I devised a plan to accompany them by shopping and having them near the casino. So, what I did was build a business that seemed safe—a bookstore that took bets in the side room, which was a café of sorts. I passed it off as a coffee shop, but waiters were also bookies. The women could bring children and grandchildren in for snacks and lunches. It worked like a charm, and we began making a lot of money. Jeff liked the way I carried the plan out and encouraged me to open other operations. So I did. Know about the shop called "For Kids Only"?

"Yeah, bought baby clothes for a friend's baby shower there," said Gail.

"Well, don't want to burst your balloon, but this too was a front. However, the store more than paid for itself. I enjoyed a very high salary from the store proceeds. On record, I'm the owner."

"Yes, I know. I'm the manager there," she said, smiling.

"Did you know about the betting?"

"Of course, but I look the other way. Like my salary, but don't need to get busted over the side room activities. What else are you involved in?"

"Not much now, since the incident concerning the politician."

"Tell me about that event."

"Well, this clown from Tupelo came in to upset all the apple carts and make a name for himself. He was actually a hardware store owner who got elected as a state rep, and he had aspirations of running for Governor but he lacked so many things, including money. He came to me because I have an Italian name and hung out in the new casinos. He thought I could and would help him. I refused, so he started playing blackjack and lost a bundle, including his hardware store. He got so upset he went to the press and blamed me for all of his stupidity. I caught him coming out of the Steak

House and knocked him out for what he'd said about me and other Italians that live here.

Later that month, after he'd blasted my name in the newspaper, he was murdered. I didn't do it and had an ironclad alibi. I was in New York at the market buying children's clothes. Three people saw and talked to me during this visit. I was exonerated, but the stigma remained. This is the reason for buying this craft. I can leave here in a hurry without going public about it. In addition, during this time, I got drafted into the Army and had to report right away," explained Tony.

"What happened to your job and business while you were away?"

"Had good managers and good bookies to keep the ball rolling on sports bets."

Gail had a strong look on her face when she asked, "When people can't pay for a bet they lost, what happens next?"

"We payoff immediately. If we are owed, we wait twenty-four hours before we contact the person who owes us. All of this is done on the phone. Should someone try to do us bad in any way, we go to him and make threats. If this doesn't work, we go to that person and physically make him understand. Not murder, but ass-kicking. Normally, this works."

"Did anyone ever find out who killed the politician?"

"Yes, someone he'd discredited in his hometown was the explanation I received.

After I returned home from the Army, a local reporter got proper information about my service in Vietnam and the medals presented to me and drafted a wonderful narrative about me. Above all, he omitted any reference to the Tupelo man. I haven't heard anything about that problem for a long time."

"What about the problem you had with Annette?"

"Well, now that is a different story. She grew up and hooked up with a Mafia made man who swore vengeance on me for her reputation being dirtied.

But I don't sweat this too much, though I do stay on guard and attentive always, and as you know, I'm packing all the time."

"You seem to have a good reputation among the folks around here. They respect and, at the same time, fear you. Did you know that?"

"No, but sorry they fear me. As the singing cowboys say, 'I'm a peaceful man.'"

"What do you want for the future?"

"Love and marriage. Open another business that is not connected to any family except mine."

"You are in your fifties now. What do you mean about such a big life change?"

They stopped for a while and let all that had been said be absorbed. Music was playing in the background, and it added drama to the situation. Finally, Gail began again, telling more about her life.

"You know, I was born in Alaska, the daughter of an Air Force pilot. We were transferred here when I was only three years old. This will always be my home. We moved to Bay St. Louis just before my dad retired. I entered school there and had a wholesome environment with family and friends who treated me very kindly. After high school, I went to Southern Mississippi on an academic scholarship. Hattiesburg was okay, but I wanted more excitement and a bigger challenge in the classroom, so I transferred to Miami without a scholarship and worked my way through. It was nice to be on my own and to endure challenges socially. I had led a restrictive life, and I met the issues and completed each obstacle with good grades.

Started off at Southern in education, but along the way, I decided not to become a teacher. Just wasn't enough money there, and I had been living on a budget all of my life. I wanted more money, so I changed to business in order to get better jobs and a larger paycheck. Got engaged just before I graduated but caught him fooling around, and we broke it off. Best thing, though—he and my dad didn't agree on anything, and this kept me upset most of the time.

I worked at a department store in Miami, but there was no opportunity for advancement, so I moved to Orlando and worked for Disney and really enjoyed it. Got promoted twice, but the cost of living there was atrocious. I was living on Ramen noodles and Spam, so when my parents learned of my existence, they came for me, and I was glad to leave and come back here, where I found a job with you."

"Yes, you did, and I'm so glad," he remarked.

They spent the night together, and the word "love" was never mentioned. Both had to report to work, and Gail had brought a change of clothing and quickly prepared herself. Tony got himself ready very early. They left together, and she took him to get his car. As they were about to depart from each other, he asked her, "Do you think we are compatible?"

She replied, "Now I do. Your compassion for Bea and Bobby has shown me a different side of you, one that I could love."

He kissed her like never before, and she walked away with her body in turmoil and her brain mixedup, but her being was saying, "I love this man and could forever."

He drove away whistling, cognizant of a deeper feeling for this woman unlike anything he'd ever known.

That evening, he had flashbacks of Hershel's story. He'd written notes for their time together in war. He pulled out his notes from an old file kept with all of his Army papers and began to assemble the story of **THE** HOT DAY IN TUSCALOOSA.

Chapter 3

As usual in the Deep South, the 4th of July was high in humidity and temperature. The Prisoners of the Tuscaloosa County Jail were assigned work details to assist county employees in preparing the streets for the annual parade.

Hershel McCoy, 19, incarcerated for theft and awaiting trial, was placed with a crew that picked up garbage and rubbish. His supervisor left him alone, and he took this occasion to escape. He knew he was innocent of the theft charges—the used lumber he was charged with had been given to him—but his family didn't know that and called the Sheriff's office. He knew he shouldn't escape, but his wife, Bea, was pregnant, and he needed to see her and take care of her needs, guessing she was with her parents, who disliked him very much. In his continued juvenile thinking, he'd just leave, see her, and take her to live with his sister, where she would be comfortable, and then he'd return to jail and get a "slap on the hand," have a trial, be released, and this would be all right.

He got in the bed of a pickup truck that he recognized as owned by a neighbor who farmed near his parents' home. The truck went north toward New Lexington, where Bea's parents lived. But it ran out of gas, and he bailed out and began running in the woods in a northern direction. After so much exertion and the temperature being so high, he fatigued and began looking for a place to hide for the evening, but for now, all he found was a brush pile in the backyard of a house located near Highway 13. He burrowed inside the pile and got some relief, but he realized it was another day of travel on foot before he found Bea. Meanwhile, he would probably be hunted by the Sheriff's department.

He was right!

The Sheriff, after learning of his escape, was torrid with rage. No one had ever done this before, and he wanted Hershel back at once, so an all-points bulletin was sent out, and nearly all his deputies were assigned to find him, including the trail dog team. A checkpoint was Jolly's store, about fourteen miles north of the city of Northport, and he was sure a squad car was in that vicinity. He'd been told horseback posses were still in vogue. But where was he to go?

Finally, he gave up on returning. He'd just take Bea and run away. His plan included, first of all, surprising her with his appearance, then getting a vehicle from somewhere near her parents' home and driving to Mississippi to live with kin who would protect them and not turn them in, and lastly, getting her medical help.

It was imperative he move faster, so he took a chance and got back on the paved road to hitch a ride. He walked about two miles before he caught a ride on a pulpwood truck driven by a Black man whom he didn't know. The ride turned at Jolly's Road, and he got out. It was only a mile from Bea's parents' home, so he had to find a place to hide. Halfway there was an old house that used stones as a foundation and was empty. He crawled under the front porch and immediately discovered the temperature was much lower. Someone used this space to store potatoes. He ate three raw ones instantly. Behind the house was an old-fashioned water well, complete with a bucket and rope. His thirst drove him out into the open to draw a bucket full. The problem was there wasn't any prime water to accomplish that. He told me later he found an old container of pickle juice and used that as a primer, which worked, and he was able to get a bucket of cool well water, which was very tasty. So some of his needs were met, and he crawled back under the house for some rest. There was nothing left to do except wait and figure out a way to contact her.

His sleep that night was fitful, with many interruptions of strange sounds. He told me later that where he was dodging the law had, at one time, been a place where skirmishes during the Civil War occurred. The story went that at one time, both sides were firing upon themselves, so folks around there deemed it a place of "Strange Battlefields." In addition, at times, sounds in the night were like cannon fire.

The next morning, as he was in a prone position, he moved up to the front of the house to scan the road. He dozed but woke up when he heard two female voices. He looked between the front steps of the porch and identified the two ladies. One was Bea, and the other was her cousin Constance. It was assumed they were on their way to the store nearby. He decided to take a chance and talk to her anyway. Before he could get out from under the building and clean up, they had disappeared; but he continued in his pursuit, went to the store,and waited outside. After a long wait, he took another chance and went in, but to his surprise, they weren't there!

Baffled at first by the look he got from Mr. Jolly, he smiled and said, "How you doing, sir? Just gonna buy a bottle of pop," then reached into the soft drink container and pulled out a Nehi grape. He paid the man and walked out without any more dialogue. He gulped the soda and jogged behind the store back to the old house. That night, a car kept driving around this area for a long time, and finally, later in the night, someone with a flashlight came onto the porch and looked inside. He waited for a long time and crawled out only when he was sure no one was there. Once he felt better about the situation, he got out and looked around. He knew then that action needed to be taken now, so he jogged a mile north up the road until he arrived at a grist mill, where a T-Model Ford was parked. There was no one around as he looked inside the vehicle. It was a crank model but without a crank, so he left it alone. He told me he was about to return to the old house when he spied a car parked behind the mill. He walked around and discovered a 1941 Plymouth that appeared to be in good shape. He looked in the front windshield and noticed the key was still in the slot.

Could he be this lucky, he thought. So he opened the driver's side, got in, and tried to get it started. No such luck. When he opened the hood and looked in at the motor, there was no battery. Across the road was a mechanic's shop, so he crossed over, looked through the front window, and discovered a battery being charged. Perhaps it was the battery from the Plymouth. In any event, it was worth a try, so he "jimmied" the door and wedged himself in, took the cables from the battery, and went outside with the battery in hand, running across the street. He placed the battery on the motor mount, hooked it up with only his fingers, and got it ready for a trial.

No such luck; the cable wasn't tight enough on the terminal. He got out and looked around the mill for tools. He found an old screwdriver and what was left of a rusty pair of pliers. He found a bent-up old can of motor oil and poured it over the pliers to make them serviceable. It worked, and he tightened the terminal cables, jumped in the car, and started it. He drove back to where he'd been staying, pulled the Plymouth into the woods on a hill, covered it with tree branches, and hurried back to the old house to get some rest, fresh water, and two raw potatoes. Tomorrow would be a big day.

The next day, early in the morning, he went to a small swimming hole near the old house and took a bath. He had no fresh clothes, so he came back a different way, crossing through two houses' backyards that had a clothesline. A pair of overalls and a white T-shirt were there, and he stole them. They didn't exactly fit, but he didn't care; he wanted to take the woman he loved away.

This time, he hid inside the house, waiting for her. Not until later did she tell him she still had morning sickness and that the only thing that would calm it was a 7UP and a grape jawbreaker. She had just enough money to buy them. Constance always bought an RC Cola and a Moon Pie.

They finally came walking on the paved road, going to Jolly's store for their objective. He lurked in some bushes in front of the old house with the idea of snatching her to come with him and travel to Mississippi.

When they came back, heading for her parents' home, he jumped out and said, "Honey, I'm so glad to see you."

She screamed, "What are you doing here?"

Hershel then told her everything—how he had been in jail, had escaped, and had been waiting for her to go with him to Mississippi. All the while, she was shaking her head and shouting, "No! No!" but he grabbed her arm and began running behind the house to the car.

Meanwhile, Constance went into convulsions and just sat down on the macadam. Bea stayed with him, and they got away for a couple of miles until that old battery stopped again. She thought she heard sirens and was glad to get out. In this part of the world, law enforcement fired first and arrested later. She was afraid for her baby and went with him into the woods for a while until they heard singing on a ridge near them.

She told Hershel she needed water, and he then pulled her in the direction of the singing, climbed the ridge, and came upon a "Brush Arbor" with homemade benches of wood slabs sitting on large rocks, eight poles planted in the ground, and a roof of pine tree branches blocking the hot sun while a Methodist preacher shouted the word of God from his Holy Bible. The entire floor was dirt. The singing of hymns was a cappella. The disruption of Hershel and Bea hushed the congregation.

During the silence, she blurted out, "Hershel McCoy, I need water at once, or I may not be able to carry this child."

He mistakenly said, "No," but this did not sit well with the preacher, who ordered Hershel, "Young man, you better get her some water right away. Our ladies will give you containers to do it with, and do it NOW."

The yelling at him turned Hershel's anger up, and he shouted back, "Who are you to talk to me that way?"

"Son, I'm your grandfather, and I know you are in a heap of trouble," said the preacher.

Hershel took two steps closer to the big older fella. "Pappaw, I'm sorry!"

"Shut up, Hershel, and get her some water."

One of the church ladies handed him a tankard and a small pail and showed him where the spring water was located. While he was gone, Bea told of his problems and how he had kidnapped her. The pastor went for his automobile and took the couple away—her home and him to the Tuscaloosa County jail.

Chapter 4

Gail and Tony, the next day, were on the phone together. Gail responded after they exchanged hellos.

"Super story about Hershel, but what I don't understand is how he got drafted since he had a pregnant wife and later a child, plus he was accused of theft and hadn't even gone to trial? Just doesn't make sense, does it?"

"No, Gail, it doesn't," he replied.

"Got another question?" she said.

"O.K., shoot," he said.

"What happened to you after you were wounded?"

"Went through some rehab but was assigned some light duty with the bravest men I've ever met—the Tunnel Rats."

"The Tunnel Rats? Tell me about them."

"I will, but let's do that over some seafood tonight. I'm in the mood for some shrimp and a pitcher of iced tea. Wanna meet me at Captain Salome's around six o'clock?"

"Yeah. May I wear shorts?"

"I'm sure I'll be jealous when you walk in; all the barflies will go crazy when they see those tan, fine legs of yours," Tony replied, kidding.

At their table in the back of Captain Salome's, they polished off two small buckets of boiled shrimp and a pitcher of draft beer, not tea.

"Now tell me about the Tunnel Rats and your job there," she asked.

"Well, first of all, my job was to be an above-ground security guard, which meant staying alert at all times and knowing where these men were located underground. It was easy duty until the Rats got in a jam. Then I did a lot of assisting. But let me tell you about them.

These guys, during the Vietnam War, came from the Australian Army and the U.S. Army, and get this—they were all volunteers who were specialist former combat engineers or from the infantry. Their job was to clear and destroy enemy tunnel complexes. Each mission meant going into dark tunnels, which were normally intricate networks the Viet Cong used, despite knowing our guys were seeking them. These tunnels were too small for the average Joe. Hell, they were only two feet by three feet, but our guys, who probably weighed no more than 130 pounds and were short, met the enemy in the dark head-on. Most of the time, they gathered valuable intelligence, supplies, and killed the enemy.

Now get this: they carried only a hunting knife, a mask, a flashlight, a small canteen of water, and, of course, a pistol with ammo in their pockets. They wore black makeup on their faces and the tops of their hands to keep the sheen from showing. Now, understand something, Gail—not only were these guys brave, but they were as cocky as Marines. They had a motto: 'Non gratum anus rodentum,' which means 'Not worth a rat's ass.'"

Both started laughing then.

"Tell me again why we had people crawling underground?" she asked.

"Always to detect booby traps and to know enemy troop presence," he answered.

"Tell you what, let's continue this at the boat. I've got some information a writer did on these men, and you'll be intrigued by what he tells. He talks a lot about the Ho Chi Minh Trail. You know who Ho Chi Minh was, don't you?" he asked.

"No, but I've heard the name," she replied.

They left and went back to the houseboat, and on the way, she let him know of her interest in the Tunnel Rats. "You know my minor was history at Miami U. Am I causing a problem, like anxiety about Vietnam?" she asked.

"No, but at one time in my life, I did experience some nightmares. I have friends who've never overcome war. Tell you what, I have some notes and historical information about the war in Vietnam, and it explains more about the Tunnel Rats."

When they returned to the boat, it hit her. "Now I know why you named the boat that crazy Latin phrase. You crazy, tongue-in-cheek type of guy," she said with a grin.

Tony went to his files and, after a bit, pulled out some papers that had started to turn yellow with age. Handing her the contents, he remarked, "Read these while I go to the store to get some coffee. Won't be long."

She nodded O.K. and began reading the information from a writer and former Tunnel Rat. Naturally, Tony had notes on all the pages. She kissed Tony and said, "Be careful and take your time, 'cause I'm a slow reader."

The first paper carried notes that said the Ho Chi Minh Trail was another name for what the V.C. called Truong Son Road. It was used as the main supply route for weapons, supplies, and, above all, the troops that were infiltrating South Vietnam. It was not just a road but a network of trails and side roads that went through eastern Laos and Cambodia to South Vietnam. The objective of U.S. troop action was to shut it down by disrupting the movement of supplies. Anyway, it cost us a lot of people, money, and a great deal of effort, using all branches of our military. But it continued to operate.

North Vietnam had people living underground for long periods of time. Why, I don't know. They seemed dumb, but their devotion to their cause superseded ignorance. You know, the only way to see or understand the difference between the V.C. and the Southern Vietnam troops was their uniforms. Hell, you couldn't trust anyone except those with round eyes. The Southern troops were known as the NVA, and there was really a difference here. The V.C. fought as guerrilla troops, while the NVA had military units in bigger numbers. Sometimes, the V.C. used villagers from the area where they attacked. The V.C. loved to attack at night and surprise you—like they did the day they first hit Hershel.

Snipers were used a lot. The best thing we could do then was to be defensive in our tactics. We'd dig in, surround ourselves with concertina wire, tie on tin cans that could make noise, place mines around our location, and sit and wait—we were the damn bait. We lost a hell of a lot of men.

I'd heard about the Tunnel Rats by then and figured this was a good idea if we could keep the brass from screwing it up. When I got assigned to them and realized my duties, I was happy. No more operating out in the open. Plus, my time in 'Nam was getting shorter.

Got there on a Sunday and was assigned a .45 pistol and leather holster with six clips of ammo. Given an area to bunk and felt comfortable so far. Met my boss, Sergeant Jarrod Black, who described my function and wanted to send me up for some training using machine guns. Still waiting on that order. My thoughts about the 'Rats are: "always on the stick." Once they have retrieved any information, equipment, or prisoners they could find, they set out to destroy the tunnel or in some way deny its use to the V.C. in the future. The hard-packed, layered clay of the tunnels made such an operation very difficult.

Early on, in the beginning, soldiers tried destroying the tunnels with conventional explosives with mixed results. Collapsing tunnel entrances by lighting a mix of acetylene gas and oxygen with small charges worked well for more shallow tunnels, but this method was too slow, inefficient, and cumbersome to use unless the area was completely secure. To deny tunnels, the 'Rats filled deeper tunnels with riot control agents like a powdered form of tear gas while collapsing the entrance with explosives. I was on detail and helped stack the outside explosives. Denial generally made the tunnels unavailable for three to six months. These deliberate operations all took time, a commodity most commanders lacked, so the tunnel rats' search was often the most important part of an anti-tunnel operation. Once done with their mission, the rats either returned to base or took a helicopter to the next tunnel in their area of operations.

Something I learned about the rats' weapons underground: While early tunnel rats entered the tunnels with M1911 .45 caliber pistols, most found the standard pistol unfit for the task. The .45 caliber round was too loud, and the muzzle flash was too bright. The rats didn't need any mechanical failures down there. Many different types of pistols were used, especially those that could use silencers; using those helped in giving crucial seconds. But this job was open to what worked best.

V.C. in the tunnels didn't surrender. In keeping silent, the sharpened bayonet was a favorite for the kill. Everybody loved their bayonet. You could use it as a probe, booby trap disarmer, and snake killer. One damn thing about a bayonet that always stuck out: it never malfunctioned or jammed.

About tunnels, I read some information written by the Vietnamese government that said: "The spectacular tunnel network stands as a testament to the endurance, wisdom, and bravery of the local people in their fight for independence." Ha! I think. Our guys and the Aussies had never lived underground as these sons ofbitches did. The NVA taught a few at the beginning, and those that followed took the training and then winged it. Yeah, we lost some good men, but I learned that later on, they held their own until the coward politicians and Generals who were after more ribbons on their coats screwed everything up. We bombed and placed artillery on those tunnels and were more than adequate. Later on, we could have dropped heavier bombs and improved our guerilla warfare to be efficient instead of being killed because they were sent to be in harm's way. Tell you one damn thing, I never met a coward tunnel rat. Nor one that would give up.

There was more, but Gail laid the papers down of Tony's war experiences. It was just too much. She wept for a long time, realizing the old expression "war is Hell" was accurate. Tony returned about thirty minutes later and came inside in a good mood.

"Hey baby, get caught up on my younger life?"

"Yeah, learned a lot, and there is more to discuss over a glass of wine."

"By the way, Gail, I'm still in the Army Reserve. We are an artillery unit, and if things get tougher in Iran or the Middle East, we could get called up. Just letting you know."

"Damn, Tony, you must have thirty years in the Reserve. You could probably retire," she said.

"Yeah, you could be right, but I am a Sergeant Major, and I'm used in the field, not administrative, so I'm needed more," said Tony.

She said, "How tall are you?"

"I'm 6 feet 2 inches tall, 208 lbs heavy. Why are you asking that?"

"Just imagining what our son would look like, you handsome devil."

"Why, Miss Gail, are you trying to tell me something?"

"Yes, I'm in love with you!"

"Well, I'll be damned, Miss Gail. How could someone as sexy as you find favor, much less love, in an old dago like me?" he said in a fake Southern accent.

"Don't ever call yourself names again. I know how polished you are, and by the way, I knew you were in the Reserve. I saw you once in uniform at the store. You looked dashing then, and I got turned on," she said with an impish grin.

"Gail, you know, you really turn me on too. Have for a while, and when I kiss you, I think I am twenty-one again. Perhaps I'm in love with you," he said with a smile.

"Do you want me to spend the night?"

"Indeed. I'll let you share my barbecue and the fixin's, plus got another bottle of wine."

"You really know how to treat a girl."

"Only when they are the best, like you."

"You silver-tongued devil."

They kissed long and sexy, then held each other on the couch and, of course, made love for a long time. When they completed their physical desires, she started asking him questions about his tour of Vietnam, Hershel, and his teen life in New York. Late that evening, they took a break and went outside to catch a breath of air. The starlight was amazing, and the ripples in the bay had a tinge of romance lingering.

Chapter 5

She went home to prepare for work at the store. Saturday was a big day, and she would be needed. Tony also had to work as a dealer that entire day at the Golden Nugget. He didn't know if it meant at a green felt Black Jack table or in the back big room doing Texas Hold'em on the red felt. He worked all day and part of the night dealing on the red felt. The house did well that night, and Tony was proud of the money he made in a week. $1,600.00 at the Golden Nugget, bonus and commission from the bookstore (gambling) earned $3,000.00 per week, Commission from the children's store earned $2,000.00, and various other activities about $1,000.00. Gail made only $250.00 per week at the children's store and $200.00 per week from the "Grannies, Moms, and Precious Ones Café." Tony had a tie-up for his paid-up houseboat at $600.00 per month, a car payment at $111.00 per month, and very little in costs for insurance and utilities. The phone was a big cost, but he could handle that. With their salaries, they could afford to marry.

For nearly a year, they romanced and talked only about marriage.

One Wednesday, Tony's day off from all work, he went home from working out at the gym to clean up and get his mail. That night, he and Gail planned to visit Biloxi and see a movie, but when Gail dropped by to see him on her way home to refresh, she walked in the door and found Tony sitting on his couch holding a pair of Army boots. At that moment, a heavy rain fell. She just sat down and looked into his brown eyes, which seemed glazed over.

"What's wrong, honey?" she asked.

He handed her an envelope from his Army reserve that stipulated the unit was being mobilized for duty in Iran.

She stood up and strolled around the boat, asking herself some questions. "How long will he be gone? Isn't he too old for the Army? Could and would he allow me to live here while he's gone? Will he be in Harm's way and get killed? Will he marry me before he leaves? Does he really love me, or does he just want to get in my panties?"

Tony arose and asked the dumbest question he'd ever uttered.

"Will you wait for me?"

"Yes. Now, are we going to a movie?"

He smiled back at her and nodded toward the door. They got in his Lincoln and took off to attempt a night of fun and forget the letter. It was over at 9:00 p.m., and he'd seen the movie before; it was *Driving Miss* Daisey" They stopped at Whataburger and enjoyed a terrific meal before going home. On the way, she started asking some of the questions she'd been thinking about. He answered most of them in one sentence when he said,

"I love you, and I want you to stay at the boat when I leave. Get rid of that junk heap you drive and keep my car. We should get married when I return and build us a house. So, I guess you'll have to make marriage plans, house-building plans, and take care of my business. I completely trust you, so I'll still have money moved into my account at the bank. I'll go to the bank, and you'll go with me for you to have access to my account to pay my bills. Now, let's go home and let me get in those panties."

She threw her head back and howled with laughter.

The next week, he took care of everything as far as business was concerned, and that Thursday, he reported at the airport to load up for New York, where they would be assigned to Fort Drum for billets and medical attention before they departed on Wednesday of the next week. All he needed to do now was gather his crews and acclimate them to who, what, when, and what they must do.

Simple, he thought, but these kids are scared to death.

My plane was extremely quiet on the way up, he thought.

He also thought about how much he already missed Gail.

Chapter 6

Another battlefield was about to be entered, he thought. He surmised it would be hotter than Nam but dusty and windy, intertwined with the heat and humidity. As he got off the MATS plane in uniform and got in formation, a jeep drove up to the platoon he was in charge of, and a Major jumped out, calling his name. He assumed the major just wanted to give him some paper instructions, but what he received was a tremendous surprise.

"Sergeant Major Gianni, I need to talk to you privately," said the major.

"Certainly, sir. Just what is it?" asked Tony.

"Let's take a walk away from here," said the Army officer.

Together they walked over behind the vehicle, and the Major then told Tony what he needed to do.

"Gianni, it has come to the Army's files that you are to be retired from the Army Reserve. You should have left three months ago. Naturally, you are not to go with this organization to Iran. Instead, here is a voucher for you to fly back to New Orleans and another voucher to rent an automobile to drive to your home in Biloxi. However, your flight will not be available until the day after tomorrow. Therefore, also in this packet is another voucher for food and a fourth one for a hotel for two nights. Also inside the packet are your retirement and discharge papers. Transportation will be available to carry you to wherever you wish to go in New York. Perhaps, when it is time for you to catch your flight, you may be able to pay that fare and get reimbursement."

"Sir, this isn't some type of joke, is it?" the astonished Italian veteran asked.

"No, Sergeant Major, not at all. Personally, I'm so glad to tell you a clerk in my office caught this and passed it on. We have contacted the Department of the Army, and they have concurred with the findings. This is a relief in many ways, but your commanding officer isn't happy about losing you. He reported you are the most qualified and experienced N.C.O. he has. Now he must change an entire firing group. Incidentally, we are detaining your regiment in order to have the retirement ceremonies for you, but I had to communicate with you now. A band is on the way here to do this right here on the tarmac."

Shortly, buses filled with Army personnel who knew how to confer this service arrived. His Company fell out and had changed uniforms for this occasion. The Major told him he would be allowed more time for this. As a rule, his family was in attendance for a function such as what was happening. He was also asked if he had any requests regarding the ceremony. His answer was not to send this to the Press for recognition. The Major certainly agreed to do that since it would make the Army Reserve look bad.

All of Ft. Drum, it seemed, turned out for the festivities. The commanding general was ashamed of the reserve unit but relieved that this middle-aged man wasn't being sent into harm's way. It was a tongue-in-cheek episode but hushed up quickly.

Tony, after the ceremonies, took a yellow cab to his parents' home in "Little Italy." They were excited about seeing him, and after learning what had happened, insisted on taking him out to celebrate.

His mother said, "We will go to Lou's Tavern tonight. Jerry Vale is performing there, and we'll make a call and explain what has happened. I'm sure they will have a table for us. They especially love to have Italians come in like us since we are 'connected,' plus we can speak the mother language."

"First, though, I gotta buy a civilian suit off the rack. I only have military clothing since I was on the way to combat," said Tony.

His dad proudly took his hero son to Sal's Clothing, where he bought two suits, one black and the other gray, plus a pair of black shoes. Naturally, Sal still carried white dress shirts with 'Mr. B.' collars. Sal waited on them himself and tossed in a free belt, socks, and underwear. Tony was set for the evening.

Anthony and Maria were so proud to show him off that evening, but an episode occurred that was as dangerous as going to Iran. He met Annette again. This, he didn't think about when it was mentioned to go out in public in Little Italy.

"Well, hello, Mrs. Gianni, so nice to see you and Mr. Gianni again. Why, Tony, where have you been?" she asked. "Haven't seen you in years. Where have you been?"

"In Vietnam," he answered and retreated to the men's room.

"She looks horrible," he thought, "and I bet she'll bring up some bad news."

When he returned to his table, she returned also and said, "Tony, may I talk to you a moment alone?"

Tony stood up and walked away with her.

"You son of a bitch, why didn't you ever contact me after I got knocked up? Don't you know we had a daughter, and now we have a grandson?"

There was fire in her eyes, and her husband was approaching. Thank God, Jerry Vale began singing again. Ironically, the song title was *You Were Always on My Mind.*

"Damn," he thought. "Another strange battlefield. I've got to get out of here. Gotta run now."

He walked over to his table, kissed his mom, and told her at the same time, "Annette is about to cause me trouble. Tell Pa why I must leave now. I will not return with y'all but must go now."

All she said was, "You sound like a hick, using words like *y'all*."

He knew where the back door was in this place and hoped it was still in the old location. Luckily, it was, and he exited immediately, took a taxi, and went to Hoboken, where he hid out in Mimi's whorehouse for a couple of days and then took a horrid bus to Atlanta. From there, he phoned Gail and told her to meet him in New Orleans. He caught a red-eye later and found Gail waiting for him in the terminal. She was baffled by all this commotion but happy to see Tony again. On the way to Biloxi and safety, he told her the wild story of what had happened to him over the last two weeks.

When they got back to the houseboat, he didn't even go outside. Instead, he grew a beard and long hair. He sent Gail to the used clothing stores and had her buy him leather and fishing boots, plus t-shirts and some long-sleeve plaid ones. He packed for two days and then purchased a good blue pickup truck to carry it all. In addition, in the front seat, hidden, were his weapons.

On a teary night, he had to say goodbye to Gail, someone he loved but, due to the deadly situation, had to leave for good. His explanation just wasn't good enough for her, but she agreed to sell the houseboat, keep the car, and go on with her life. He could never tell her where he was going or when he'd return. He gave her letters to send to various people to end him in all businesses in Southern Mississippi. It was going to cost him a fortune but perhaps could keep him alive. He went to a pay phone and contacted his parents, telling them he'd try to be in touch on Christmas each year. He asked for prayer and to avoid Annette. He knew her family wanted him dead. He did ask them to find out about his grandchildren but to make no contact. He'd do that himself but didn't know where or when. He left, heading north to the Ozark Mountains, to a destination he wasn't sure of.

Two months later, Gail was shot and killed in his car while parked at a Walmart store in Pass Christian. He learned about this much later. Upon getting this news, he deemed her a casualty of another "Strange Battlefield." He grieved and was deeply saddened. He had tried to phone her at her parents' home when he had settled but didn't reach her or hear of her death until he called her old job at the children's clothing shop, and her replacement reported the sad news.

Chapter 7

In the northern part of Arkansas, at its most rugged vicinity, was a community named Cripple Creek. There was a fishing cabin he'd won in a poker game, plus a lot of local land, but he had visited there only once. On that visit, he remembered the cabin was on the northern banks of the White River. While there, he went to a courthouse to finish up ownership papers that had been transferred over to him. Annually, he was billed for taxes, which he paid right on time. He found the keys to the cabin in his desk and placed them on his truck's key ring.

The night he left Biloxi, he told no one, not even Gail. She had returned to live with her parents until Tony sent for her. He got on the interstate and drove straight to Jonesboro, Arkansas, before he rested. He spent two days at a motel near Arkansas State University, where he bought a cap as evidence, he thought, of his tie-in to the region.

He vaguely remembered how to reach this obscure village in the White River area. He couldn't even remember where the town was that held the county seat, so he just drove until he recognized any obscure landmark. He did—a very tall mountain north of the village. As luck would have it, the petrol remaining in the truck was getting low. He had to find a gas pump somewhere, and then he would ask where the village of Cripple Creek was located.

After traveling a winding road that was now getting steeper by the mile, he topped off and started downhill. He put the gear in neutral and began to coast in order to save gasoline when he saw a store on the left side of the highway. When he hit bottom, he braked, put the truck back into gear, and pulled over to the ESSO pumps in front of Casey's General Store.

He stepped out of the truck, and a short, middle-aged man stepped out the front door with no excited salutations. All the mountain man said was, "Whut kin I do fer you, feller?"

Tony answered, "Fill it up."

Not another word was spoken. Tony went into the store and paid the man twenty-five dollars and two cents. No "thank you" or "come back" or anything else, so Tony asked, "How do you get to White River Road from here?"

"Whatcha want to go thur fer?" asked the gas-pumping man.

"Own a cabin there and want to use it," answered Tony.

"Ya mean you own a place and don't know how to find it?" he asked, somewhat incredulous.

Tony was tired and put out with this man when he answered, "Hell yes. I've only been there once in my life, and it has been a few years back, so kindly tell me how to locate that road."

"Can't get thur from heah. Gotta get somebody to show ye," the man answered. "By the way, ye gotta name?"

Tony replied, "Damn right, but you didn't tell me your name, and before I tell you mine, tell me yours."

"Hell, Yankee feller, hits on the sign outside. Hits Casey."

"Mine's Anthony Gianni," said Tony.

Casey started laughing and said, "Let me lock up, and I'll take you to your cabin, Mr. Anthony. And by the way, you'd be better off getting some supplies. There is no other store around here, and sure as hell, the cabin has no 'lectric power, and dem squirrels probably dun et the 'lectric lines up. Shore, you gonna need sum kerosene lamps, plus water in dem damn bottles, and some grub ye can chomp on 'stead of cookin'. Got matches 'r a cigarette lighter?

'Cause if'n you don't, you're gonna freeze your ass off without heat."

Tony just grinned at the man and said, "Well, fix me up with what I need."

Casey got busy then and filled an order of survival—except fishing bait.

"Mr. Anthony, ye know how to fish wid a fly fish way?"

"Yes, I do, Mr. Casey, but put in an assortment of flies. I have tackle."

"Okay, will do, suh, and I'll load you up. Thais is gonna cost you forty-seven dollars even. Don't like to fool with change until I gets to know you bettah. You might expect a Yankee dime, and I don't keep them. So if'n you gonna stay heah fer a long time, we'll just round everything off."

Tony paid him in cash. Casey locked up, got into his old pickup, led him about a mile down the road, and turned right onto a crooked, muddy road until they found the creek.

Arrival at the cabin was no big deal, but it looked better than expected. Tony noticed the windows had been replaced, garbage was outside, and a few empty whiskey bottles were on the porch.

"Looks like somebody has been here lately. Know anything about that, Mr. Casey?"

Casey got in his truck, turned around, and headed out, shouting out his window, "Dem teenagers know how to get up heah," then departed.

The front door was unlocked, so he went in, afraid this wasn't the same cabin. But he strolled around the place and realized this was his cabin, and somebody had invaded it. He unloaded his provisions and what he'd brought up from Biloxi and Jonesboro.

The place had a rebuilt fireplace, and he went outside to gather firewood.

At the back of the cabin was a big pile of freshly cut firewood. Now he really was suspicious. Teenagers didn't saw firewood because they wouldn't stay more than a day. Fishermen were the likely poachers.

He got a broom that Casey had placed on the order list, swept the entire place out, built a fire in the fireplace, and put a zip-up sleeping bag on one of the beds near the heat. His cooler, with melted ice but loaded with various drinks, was on the porch. He boxed up what he'd bought from Casey and placed it in a wooden box in his attempt to protect the contents from varmints, especially bears. He took his revolvers, ammo, rifle, and bow and arrows and placed them on the rafters.

He slept that night, but the sounds of the Ozarks vibrated through the cabin like a bad Little Richard record.

The next morning, he checked outside and noticed the porch had been visited by raccoons or squirrels. Too much debris was strewn on the steps. He gave himself a mental note to build a fire outside to avoid leaving the impression that a human was inviting them to attempt entering the cabin. A fire outside, away from the building, could deter them from any such notion.

He also remembered that when he was once trapping out west, he played his transistor radio all night to make the critters think he was awake and aware of their presence.

He needed to return to Casey's General Merchandise for some additional personal things. His concern from Casey was whether he knew of anyone who had been using the cabin other than teenagers. He also needed an Arkansas road map in order to determine which direction to find someone who could come to the cabin for a rebuild, remove this one, or erect a brand-new building.

But first, he needed utilities spotted and connected. He also wanted phone service of some type and TV antenna service.

It was time to square up with Casey.

He pulled up in front of the store—not by the gas pump—got out, and went in to have a one-on-one with the owner.

"Good morning, Mr. Casey," he said as he went in.

"Mr. Anthony," answered Casey.

"I need to tell you a few things, sir," said Tony.

"Yes, sir, go right on ahead," answered Casey.

"I'm actually moving into my cabin. I'm going to buy a few pieces of furniture, and I also need to find someone who is a contractor to help me. I'm retired, but I will do more than fly fish. I plan to eventually build other cabins on my property that will be standard type. I noticed there is a drug store connected. Is it useful, or has the owner left here?"

"Mr. Anthony, you must have some money to do all this. Yes, I know a contractor who can fix your cabin now, but I don't think he'd be interested in home building. He lives in Fayetteville, and you can ask him, but hell's bells, don't you think you need to get electricity done first? And what're you gonna do about sewage? You can have a septic tank done now, but if you build those homes for sale or rent, you're gonna have to do a lot more utilities, I reckon."

"True on all accounts, sir," answered Tony.

"I'd welcome you building other homes—good for my business. We have another store here that wants to open up more than one day a week. Sells antiques but don't have a place to live, though. Maybe you could sell them one of yours."

"Perhaps I could, but my theme would be a house on the riverbank with a pier and walkway from the house to the water," answered Tony. "They would cost a pretty penny. I'm prepared to build streets connecting them to each other and to the highway."

"Feller, this ain't no town, just a village. You're gonna need a whole lot of other things to do what you're talkin' about," stated Casey.

"If there was a town here, I'd open a few shops to help the population."

Casey just looked at him with big eyes and said, "Why would you wanna do that?"

"Progress. Who said all of this would make life better? Our ancestors did just that," said Tony.

"Yeah, but they didn't have a lot of people in Little Rock not wanting the little man to get any bigger," said Casey in a raised voice.

"I'm sure they didn't, but if they hadn't tried... I spent over a year as a soldier in Vietnam, and if I hadn't tried to live, I wouldn't be here."

"Folks movin' in here will change our way of life, wouldn't it?" he asked.

"Yeah, it would, but it will be better," replied Tony.

"Have you ever changed your life?" asked Casey.

"Many times. Home, where I was born and raised, changed and hid me. Folks, as you say, are always trying to destroy me, but I don't give in. I am a survivor," he said.

"Seems to me ye wanna be a builder too," stated Casey.

"Guess that is true. I'd like to always make my environment get better," said Tony.

"Sir, what does 'environment' mean?" asked the mountain man.

"Means your surroundings," taught Tony.

"I'll be damn, heered that word all my life and didn't know what it meant, and come to find out I really did know all the time—afraid, though, it meant sumpin else."

"Please tell me the name of the guy you recommend, and I'll take first things first. I'll get a cesspool dug and have the utility line extended to electrify my home. In the process, I'll decide what to do with the existing structure. Now, what's his name?"

"Oh, sorry, it's Pete Oats. He lives up in the holler, but I have his phone number. You can call from heah if'n ye wanna."

He called immediately, and Pete agreed to meet him at his cabin so they could talk. Casey said the county was dry, and he didn't sell likker any mo' but it weren't fer away to the next county to get some hard drink plus beer and wine.

Tony asked the store owner, "How did you know I wanted to buy some drink?"

"Shoot, feller, you from city, and all city folk I know, loves to get likkered up," answered Casey.

"Well, do you like to take a drink?" Tony asked.

"Shore do, likes my beers too," said Casey.

They both laughed.

"Hey Casey, when I go to buy some stock, want me to pick up something for you?"

Casey reached into the bib of his overalls, pulled out a big wad of cash, peeled off a twenty-dollar bill, and said, "Git me some of that vodkee, you cain't smell dat stuff, dem ruskies that makes it know how to take taste out ofit. Hear tell dat stuff is made by taters and sometimes by sugah cane."

It started to rain, so Tony went back home and waited on Pete.

An hour later, Pete came driving up in a logging truck. After they shook hands, Pete entered the cabin.

"Mr. Anthony, this shell ain't nothin' but plywood and nails. Lumber here is pine from downstate. If I was you, I'd tear it down, use the wood saved would be used to build a pier, and I'd do a brick or stone home. Site is okay, but after we settle on the way you want the front to face, get the cesspool dug and built, have electricity run from the highway up here, and have water pipes dug and set. You'll have to get your water from the spring, which is about forty yards from this location. I can do that fer you and save you some money. By the way, how you gonna finance this home?"

"VA," said Tony.

"Go to First Bank of Fayetteville, see Mr. West, and tell him I sent you. We'll get started as soon as you see the banker and the utility people. I have a friend that can give you a good price on a septic tank. By the way, I have three cedar trees we're cutting, and I'll contact a rock masonry in Branson to learn if he has enough rock and Masons available to get the job done. Don't know if anyone has told you, but we don't have cell phone service available now, so you're going to have to contact the phone company when it's time to connect to a landline. Actually, it would be okay to get the phone hooked up as soon as possible in order for all of us to communicate," said Pete.

"Right. I'll get that done after I go to the bank. Meanwhile, would you get in touch with your man that does septic tanks?" asked Tony.

"Sure, and will get you a price. Here is my card with my number, so as soon as you get everything done in Fayetteville and call me, I'll begin," stated Pete.

Chapter 8

Tony built a fire in the barren fire pit with some coal he found on the creek bank and covered it with semi-wet leaves to create smoke that the critters might think meant people were home in this cabin. He called Mr. West from the bank for an appointment the next day. It was granted for two o'clock at the bank. He sought a debit card from there after he opened an account. In the meantime, he took a different route to the next little town to buy a case of beer, a bottle of bourbon, and two bottles of vodka. He returned that evening, dropped off the bottle of vodka the Ruskies made, and returned to his fire pit to restoke it. He had bought a sack of hamburgers from McDonald's, so he had dinner.

After his meal, he rummaged through his paperwork and found that Gail had hired an architect from Biloxi that indicated exactly did as she had requested. It was one he wanted also. He made a mental note to write it on the paper attached to the blueprint to get enough money to pave the road from the highway to his house. Since he really didn't know how, he'd hire some locals to make him a garden next spring with plenty of vegetables. He'd have to cover it with plastic to keep the varmints out. Smiling at this idea, he knew he'd have to build a barn somewhere next to his existing property.

He prepared for the evening and stored his beer in the creek in a Styrofoam container that would keep the brews cool.

The next morning, early, he went west to Fayetteville to do a lot of business. He had brought all of his money in three briefcases that amounted to almost a million dollars. He had more money in different banks located in New Orleans, plus stocks and bonds that amounted to more than a million dollars with his broker in Pascagoula. His lawyer was there too, holding his will and other important papers. He was in good shape, but he would never return to the Gulf Coast again, and no one other than his attorney could ever know his whereabouts. His parents didn't know anything either, though they had met his attorney before, but it was doubtful they'd remember his name.

His first venture was locating a paving company and making a deal to get started next week. Next to the paving business was Lowe's. He went in at eleven a.m. and exited at one o'clock, having bought an entire kitchen, washer and dryer, John Deere riding lawn mower, weed eater, a complete set of DeWalt tools, a chainsaw, wall lamps, and some ceiling lamps that included cooling fans. After showing the manager his plans, he bought carpet for the entire house, a television large enough to cover a wall, and got the name of the best landscaper. He paid cash for everything and, after giving directions to his soon-to-be-built house, told them not to do anything but wait for his phone call. He then left for the utility office and paid to have the lights turned on immediately. He got favorable attention there.

After lunch—a steak with trimmings—he headed to the bank for his appointment. Realizing he was still early, he entered a barber/beauty shop and got the "max," which included a hair wash, razor trim, manicure, and pedicure. Then he crossed the road and went into the bank to meet Mr. West.

"Yessir, glad to meet you, Mr. Gianni, or is it Mr. Anthony?" said Bill West.

"It's Gianni. I did that to Mr. Casey because he tried to learn too much about me, and it wasn't any of his business."

West laughed at that and said, "I know what you mean. Now, what must I do to be of help to you?"

"I own property across the road from Casey's store on the creek bank, and I wish to build a very nice home there, using my G.I. Bill to finance it. Here are my floor plans and the estimated cost of construction. I have already paid to have my driveway paved, utilities connected, a septic tank dug, kitchen furniture purchased, and a phone installed. I plan on building a barn near the property and will demolish the existing cabin, using the remaining wood to have a pier and pier house built later on the creek bank. Pete Oats will be my construction director and will begin the demolishing and pier building almost same time. Hope to start Thursday of next week. Land phone installed in two days and septic tank is being handled now.........This design doesn't leave any margin for error, so on the day for' 'close out' I'll be busy on job site.

"Mr. West, do you have your VA connection and discharge papers from the Army?"

"Yes, on both. If I'm not mistaken, there will be fees associated with the construction. I wish to open an account here with a large deposit. Deduct any necessary fees from my account. I also want a debit card, a credit card, and paper checks." He handed West proof of his stocks and bonds, property ownership, and evidence of the land where the house would be built.

Mr. West said, "This will expedite matters tremendously. I must run this loan through the G.I. Bill and get investor approval."

"I was sure of this, but I've experienced that most bankers are slow in their paperwork. I want this loan approved in two weeks."

"No, sir, it's just not that fast," West said, growing erratic.

"In two weeks, no less," Tony said.

"What's your hurry?" West asked, a determined look on his face.

"I need to move in as soon as possible. I plan on using my cash to build six waterfront homes for resale once mine is complete. I have connections in Bull Shores to bring in fly fishermen and their families. Quite frankly, sir, we need to turn this village into a city. We'll need churches, a satellite bank, schools, eateries, a grocery store, and some kind of medical facility. I'll be living in this house for the remainder of my life. If you want to work with me concerning building my house during the time I've requested, great but otherwise if you don't then I'll go to another bank. Old expression, time is money. I'm about to spend a lot of money here. Therefore, I'll need an answer as soon as possible.   West stood up and in a loud le

"leader" type voice bellowed, "Hold on sir, you've given me a large undertaking". Let me at least call in my committee and explain something about you and what you are planning." They are going to ask a lot of questions to which I don't have answers that is satisfactory. One being, I don't even know you myself"

Mr. West, that isn't important, but I'll tell you a few things about me that you could find out easily enough. I'm from Biloxi, Mississippi, where I owned three businesses that were highly profitable. I was moved to New York to be sent to Iran for battle when a clerk in personnel found out I was too old to remain in the Army, so I was retired. I went back to Biloxi, sold everything I owned, and decided to move here because I had won the cabin and property in a poker game. I had visited the cabin once before and liked it. I enjoy fly fishing, and since I am not married, it was ideal for me to move into this area of our country.

I didn't need to live on the Gulf Coast anymore—too many hurricanes and tornadoes. I'm willing to open a couple of stores in Cripple Creek to contribute to the possible idea of expanding into a city rather than remaining a village. My taxes from the house sales, plus from the stores, will enable us to see a future here. I need your help in securing support from the political people and your people to work with me on this.

"Well, we'll see what I can do. Do you have a number I can contact you at?" said the bank president.

"For the time being, call Casey's number, and he'll send for me. Do you have his number?"

"Yes, I'm sure I do. By the way, in a situation like this, we'll need to get your credit listing. Should I contact Biloxi?"

"Indeed, they are prepared to give you my information," said Tony.

"Our state representative can help you push this through, and I'm thinking all of this will be done within a week if you'll use fax. When I get my phone, I will get one of those to use in my work."

West was about Tony's age, and he could size up people very well. When he saw Tony walk out of the bank, he knew this was a leader and would be good for his bank. Proof of cash was big in his assumptions.

Tony left and went to the Bass Pro Shop and bought a boat, a Mercury motor, and a trailer, hooked it up to his truck, and headed back to Cripple Creek. He'd spent a bunch of money today but was glad about what he'd done. His future looked bright, and he was so happy he'd made that bank President squirm.

Casey came outside to look at Tony's boat. "Well, sir, got yourself a nice 'un. Need oil and gas?"

"Yep, I'll take a spin to try it out," said Tony.

He went inside and phoned Pete, who told him the friend who did septic tanks would be there Saturday to get the job done. "You can pay him then, and y'all can mark the spot according to the blueprint you have. I need to come over to stake out the location tomorrow morning, though. What would be the best time?"

"Nine would be fine. Got a new boat today, and I'm guessing you've been up and down the stream many times, so when you get here, maybe we can take her out."

"Sure, would love to," said Tony.

Casey came back in and asked Tony if he needed soft drinks or a cooler.

"Need both," exclaimed Tony. "You know, you're getting like that guy on *Green Acres* who is always trying to sell something—you know, Mr. Haney."

Casey said, "Don't get many people in heah dat have walkin' around money like ye do."

Both men laughed, and each realized the other was fast becoming a friend. Tony bought some chain and a lock to secure the boat to a tree in his front yard. Casey threw in some rope to tie it down when the weather got bad.

"Yep," Tony said to himself, "we must be friends—he gave me something free."

In no time at all, the septic tank was dug and placed, the house was laid out, PVC pipes for the bathrooms and kitchen were set for the future, the road was paved, and the house pier was built from former cabin materials. Tony paid him up front for the staking, destruction of the cabin, and building of the house pier, since Pete had to hire a plumber for this project. He was going to use the cedar planks from Pete, but Rock Masons, rocks, concrete, and intricate carpenter work would fall under the G.I. Bill funding. The other building crew was known as Bull Shoals Builders and was highly recommended. Their owner was Stella Sands.

He finally got the electricity hooked up to a main line. The phone line was now intact, and the number was (333) 383-1771. Casey phoned him the morning after the phone man had departed and said that Mr. West had called, seeking information about Tony, and asked if he would contact the new resident and have him call the bank.

Tony called Mr. West and was told by the receptionist that Mr. West was en route to Cripple Creek to see Tony with three other people who wished to meet him, so he respectfully requested that he remain at his land site. Tony agreed and went to his campsite on the house pier. He had placed a cot there for sleeping, bathed in the creek, and used the woods for bathroom activities. His clothing hung on a wire near his fireplace. It was strange looking—a paved road, campsite, pier, septic tank, staked area, and wires hanging down from new poles.

After these visitors departed, he was going to Fayetteville to a furniture store to select furniture. He felt strange doing this and needed Gail to assist him. It had been a month since he had seen her, and he missed her terribly.

It was a cloudy day but warm when West came driving in on the new road in a black SUV of some brand and pulled up to where Tony had set up chairs and a small fire blazing with a pot of coffee brewing. Cups and saucers were on display. Plastic spoons, packages of sugar, and cream were on a pile of paper napkins, all bought from Casey's store.

Mr. West got out from the driver's side, and two other folks got out. One was a very pretty lady in tight blue jeans, cowgirl boots, and a satin blue cowgirl top, with blonde hair and brown eyes. He was impressed. The other passenger was also in jeans but wore engineer boots, a red and black plaid shirt, and had a rugged look.

"Good morning, Mr. Gianni. Sorry to barge in on you without an appointment, but I wanted you to meet these fine young people. First, this is Ms. Stella Sands of Bull Shoals Builders, and this is our U.S. State Representative, Jeff Powers."

Handshakes went around, and Tony offered coffee. All sat down with their refreshments.

Bill West opened the meeting by saying, "Sir, I'm sure you wonder why I'm here and why I brought these two wonderful people to meet you today. Most Saturdays are for playing, not meeting about business. However, I had to speak to you today, and these people were available. They are on our board, so that partially explains their appearance.

"Ms. Sands owns the business you want to erect and modify your new home. I told her of your plan to build a riverside housing development."

"Mr. Gianni, I find your idea provocative and not in the least nefarious. I think if land is available on the banks of the White River, it would behoove all of us here to invest our talents, motivations, and money to profit greatly."

"Sir," said Jeff Powers, "we think, and I believe you would agree, that in order to make this a success, we need to build a city to entice buyers for the many homes we could erect here."

Chapter 9

"What in hell are you people thinking? Build a city? **Silence** But! But! You'll need roads, business buildings, schools, churches, and land, plus leadership to tackle an undertaking like this," said Tony.

"Correct," said Bill West, "and that is why we are all here. But let me ask you, sir, what would you do first if you had the opportunity in this village?"

"Buy all the land I could, stake it out in the town square, offer lots at various prices throughout. Contact the state and have the Governor pass an amendment to change this from a village into a city. Push somebody in Little Rock to get, for this so-called new city, streets, water, electricity, law enforcement, a fire department, a medical facility of some kind, merchants, small industry, and streetlights. Promote what has been done and go after people to live here. Promote fly fishing—hell, I'd open a business that sold products and taught fly fishing. We need restaurants that offer different menus. Ms. Sands should have her company begin as soon as possible in building six new homes like mine on the river and offer them to people who live in other areas and will just visit occasionally to be our testing board. Build the city first and then start on additional land with less expensive homes. Gotta have a bank that specializes in home loans."

West was beaming when he said, "You left one thing out, Mr. Gianni."

"What's that, Mr. West?"

"Leadership… A Mayor and city council. We recommend that you should be the Mayor, and we would further recommend Casey Powers as a council member, along with two people you haven't met: Mr. Todd Nixon, the person who owns our drug store that is partially opened, and Dr. Elizabeth Sanders, our veterinarian. All of the council members have great traits—common sense, sensitivity, non-radical, and love for this area.

"Now, let me explain someone to you who isn't what you think he is—the person you met, Casey Powers. The hillbilly act isn't Casey. Before he opened the General Store, he was a principal of a high school in Harrison. This is just an act to learn more about you and a few other people until they figure him out. His son is this man here," he said, pointing his finger at Jeff Powers.

Tony said loudly, "GOT ME! But Jeff, I'm going to get him back in some way," he said, laughing.

The entire bunch of people laughed even harder as Casey walked up. Jeff said, "Daddy, knock it off with the hillbilly act on Tony. He's good people. Now, not being disrespectful, but leave here for now. We are in a meeting but will see you before I return to see your grandchildren."

"Oh! Sorry, thought y'all were in Tony's new boat," said Casey.

"Liar! Liar! Pants on fire," said Bill.

He departed, walking back to his store, laughing all the way.

Jeff then spoke up, "What do you think about this wild idea, Tony?"

"You folks are unbelievable, wild, and maybe perfect. Yes, I'll be your Mayor but why didn't you select one of the council members?"

"Casey loves the idea of a city, but to him, it's just a hobby having a store here. Being a Mayor in his estimation, would tie him down. He'd much rather be in your boat, fishing for nothing—just floating. Todd wants the drug store opened again, but when it does, he says he'd only be available on the nights he meets with Mayor and council. Elizabeth is just too busy. She'll have to make time even to attend council meetings."

Chapter 10

"But why me? Y'all have only known me for hours instead of days. You don't know anything about me, and just because I told a banker I'd love to see this village become a city isn't any reason to bring up something that couldn't ever become much more than a lot of nothing if pursued," said Tony.

"Well said, sir, but you are very wrong about our knowledge of you. For example," Bill West said as he pulled papers from his briefcase and began reading, "You are from New York City, went to Fordham, and, for reasons we haven't learned, moved alone to Biloxi, Mississippi, where you worked as a croupier in casinos. In time, you bought and built three profitable businesses. You got drafted and sent to Vietnam, where you were shot but came back and became a hero. You returned to Biloxi, kept your three businesses, enriched them, and, on the side, worked as a gambler, where you won a lot of cash and properties like the one you won here. You retired for reasons we haven't found out. You are rich and kind, people say. The Governor of Mississippi thinks you are awesome, and the Governor of Arkansas wishes to meet you. He says he wants to meet a bona fide hero and a Mayor of this city. He requests that you have a festival or something as soon as possible," said Bill West.

"You've got to be kidding. Mike Huckabee, a fine Governor and even better man, I understand, is willing to appoint me Mayor based on the little information all of you have to build a city. That's correct, and all of us will help you. I said I'd do it because I knew in advance that the Governor would have a hand in this and will probably throw me out once he really gets to know more about me. It is so ludicrous just to think I could actually do this," said Tony.

"Well, maybe that's true, but just being an authorized gambler doesn't make you one of the bad guys. You have no criminal record, so we stand by what we've said and what we want. We want a man of action as our leader, and that's you," said Jeff.

"Assuming all of this works out, when do I go to Little Rock to be sworn in?" asked Tony.

"You don't. He comes here to meet you and will do the chore," said Ms. Sands.

"I suggest we have some type of activity while he is here and invite some prospects to meet you and the Governor." Said Bill West.

"Well, do you have a date yet? About this festival, what is the theme?If we invite people to come here and they are prospects, don't y'all think my house should be finished so they may take a tour to realize what their house will look like? Doesn't the river look like it needs at least some dredging work?" said Tony. He continued, "Jeff, first things first."

"Ms. Sands, assuming we must set a date in a month, can you have the house finished by then?" asked the excited Mr. Powers.

"No, we will need time for the rock to set. Probably in two months. Next, let's build a temporary city hall," she continued, seemingly providing logic to the conversation.

"I concur with Mr. Gianni about having this place cleaned before we begin. Jeff, get the Corps of Engineers up here to at least sow grass and remove the dead trees and roots from the stream," the nice lady said. "While you are at it, Jeff, how about building a holding pond for trout in the future? If I was asked or even considering moving here, I'd want to know what it would be like in ten years at least. I'd be impressed knowing fish would be available in the future. And Jeff, while we are talking about buildings in Cripple Creek, a branch office/storage would add to the look of the city. Don't you agree, Mr. Mayor?"

"Yes, Ms. Sands, I do, plus buildings for the fire department and police department," Tony said.

Keeping in the spirit of it all, Tony began his own questions. "Does the village own any properties within the city limits?"

"Yes," said Jeff. "I'll get my dad to show us exactly where they are located."

"Speaking of city limits, are there any documents that tell us where they are located?" asked Tony.

"Yes, at the county seat," replied Bill West.

"Tell you what, don't anybody except Ms. Sands do anything until we have those documents in our hands. Don't anybody do anything until the Governor does his work. Jeff, secure from your father any and all documents he possesses. Nothing personal, just city business. Remember, all, once I'm sworn in, your days of involvement will begin and end with me."

Ms. Sanders motioned for Tony to join her as the group was heading for the vehicle. When he neared her, she looked directly into his eyes, smiled, winked, and said, "I'll have a crew here on Monday. Just show them where and talk to the foreman, then leave to do other things," she said.

"But the loan hasn't been approved," said Tony.

"Oh yes, it has. I have someone in Little Rock that works for the VA benefit program who tells me all is okay."

Tony smiled and waved them all goodbye. She winked again.

On Sunday, Casey brought Tony a homemade plate of fried chicken complete with all the fixings and told him that as soon as the city hall was finished, he'd bring all city papers over. Tony mentioned that when the plans were drawn up, he'd include offices for the council. Casey liked that idea. That same day, Pete brought two truckloads of cedar lumber and piled it near the staked-out area for the workers to begin soon. Tony went fishing while the lumber was delivered and didn't see Pete.

The next day, he was requested to come to the bank and sign the G.I. loan papers and close out all paperwork. While filling up his truck with gas, he saw Pete enter the store. He followed him in and asked him to come to his truck for some business. Pete returned with two cups of coffee later, and Tony asked him to get his bills so he could pay him. Of course, this pleased Pete. The lumber, demolishing of the cabin, and building of the house/pier were all he owed, but in his memory bank, he knew he'd use Pete in years to come.

To his surprise, Bull Shoals Builders' crew of carpenters and plumbers arrived as he was talking to Pete, so he returned to the house site to meet with the foreman, named Roman Pasqual.

"Sir, I understand you are going to build yourself a city?"

"No, the Governor and the people here are doing that. I shall just be another steward with the title of Mayor." answered Tony.

"I assume, sir, these stakes represent where you wish to have your house built?" asked Mr. Pasquel.

"Sir, your assumption is correct," answered Tony.

"Very elaborate floor plan, sir. Your architect did a great job, it seems," Pascal commented.

"Thank you. It was a dream house that I conferred to him, and this is his final presentation," said Tony.

"Very well, sir. We should follow it with care, but of course, you are welcome to visit at any time. We aim to please, and Ms. Sands instructed and indoctrinated us to follow your lead in any measure you deem worthy and becoming," said Pascal.

"Indeed. She appears to me to be a woman of definitive thoughts. What is her husband like?" said Tony.

"She is adjustable and not obstinate when the other person has an ideal and idea as you do. She isn't married. Are you?"

"No."

"Very well, I must begin. Am I correct in my assumption that the lumber stacked here is what we are to use?"

"Yes," answered Tony.

"Wonderful aroma—cedar, right?" asked Pascal.

"Yes, cut here by Pete Oats," answered Tony.

"Know him well. Know he cuts according to measurements. Did he see this blueprint?" asked the foreman.

"Yes, and he allowed for your needs should the occasion require. Not to worry, I bought all the logs this came from so as not to be caught shorthanded. I'll be living in the house on the pier until you finish. Be aware, the electricity is 'hot.' A septic tank has been dug, but the water hasn't been established yet. No water line on this side of the highway, according to Casey, but we may cut through the highway and connect with the water lines on that side. We should have it run over here by the time you need water connections. I'll contact the water department in Fayetteville to get the problem resolved. When we can, we'll buy the rights and establish our own water department."

"Yes, the Governor wants me to be happy," he said with a smile. "Guess I'll go and phone the water people in Fayetteville now," said Tony.

"Sir, I don't mean to intrude, but I know the people there and may be able to alleviate the problem quicker. And as a resident of Cripple Creek, I'd like to volunteer to do this for you and the city."

"Proceed, Mr. Pascal, but keep me informed. Please keep me informed at all times."

As Tony was walking to his truck, he was glad this man was on the job. He thought then, *I've recently entered another strange battlefield. Being a* Mayor is *going to give me more anxiety and stress. Why did I say I would?* But he got in his truck and drove to the bank to sign his papers to pay for his house being built.

It was done in a lawyer's office. A representative from the bank was present, carrying an armful of loan papers. Afterward, he treated himself to a meal of prime rib, baked potato, salad, and draft beer. He bought a pair of blue jeans and a denim shirt at Sam's, and as he was walking outside, he noticed a man sitting on the bed of his pickup. The man had a sign and a cage that held brown boxer puppies.

The sign said:PURE Boxers. $80.00.

He was getting lonely in the evenings. He had been calling Gail at various times but got no answer. He'd call her tonight and tell her about the dog. So, he made the deal and bought "Toby," a handsome, masculine-looking dog. They hit it off at once.

Little did he know at this time, but before the night would end, this animal would solve a lot of grief destined for him in this strange battlefield.

He stopped at Casey's just as he was closing and bought a case of water, a big bag of puppy chow, a collar, food dishes, a chain, and a snap. He also had Casey take a picture of Toby and himself. He planned to mail this picture to Gail. Her phone had been disconnected, and it bothered him. In the letter, he would leave his new number so she could call him.

Monday morning, he would take Toby to Dr. Sanders. He wanted to meet Elizabeth anyway.

That twilight, as the concrete truck was leaving after pouring the flooring, steps, and patio trim, Tony looked around at what had been satisfactorily completed. He got himself a snack, a beer, and a bath. Then, he called the home of Gail's parents. He hesitated in doing this because he felt the older couple didn't like him.

After three rings, Colonel Cameron answered the phone, and the conversation became awkward from the beginning.

"Colonel Cameron speaking."

"Sir, this is Tony Gianni, trying to find Gail. Could you tell me her new number?"

There was a long pause, and Tony kept saying, "Sir? Hello, sir?"

"Tony, I assume you haven't been told, and I regret telling you, but Gail was shot to death about a month ago. She was driving the car you gave her, and the assassin nearly shot her lovely face away. We couldn't open the casket for viewing at the funeral—it was so grotesque. The police have been trying to find you to learn if you have any idea who did this horrible thing."

"Sir, I am so sorry, so sorry," he began to weep. Then, composing himself, he said, "I don't know who did this, and I'll phone the police and inform them of that fact. Colonel, I know you and Mrs. Cameron are grieving, and now I am. Sir, I loved her, and we were planning on marriage and a family."

"Oh, Tony, I have no malice toward you, and I'm sorry this has happened to you as well. Guess none of us will ever be the same again. Where are you—in Iran?"

"No, sir, and I'm not permitted to tell my location. You understand, don't you, sir?"

The Colonel, assuming Tony was back in the Army, dropped the subject.

"Tony, when you get back, come by and see Nellie and me. Again, son, I'm sorry for you."

"Yes, I want to express my condolences to all of your family. Goodbye."

He picked up Toby and held him in his arms as he wept. He looked down at the note he had written to insert in the letter with the picture, but now there was no one to send it to.

That night, after five shots of bourbon, he fell asleep around midnight.

The next morning, he had a tremendous hangover. He put on his bathing trunks, drank a Sprite, took a pain pill he had kept from Vietnam or somewhere, and jumped into White River. If the pill killed him, he didn't care.

Gail was the only woman he had ever loved. He had been missing her, but now that would increase. Coupled with grief, it gave him no return, he thought.

In the water, he remembered his duties, and he was not someone to shirk responsibilities—especially those as Mayor of a city being built. He had to suck it up and continue.

This Sunday, he planned on a trip to Fayetteville to attend Mass. He needed solace and, later, more profundity—like what he had gained from Gail. Perhaps he could receive this in church.

The splash in the cold waters of White River brought him around from the hangover, and he was hungry. He put on his new clothing and hopped in his truck for a trip to Casey's Store for breakfast. Alice, a middle-aged lady, operated an area in the store that could be declared a deli. Only breakfast and lunch were available on the menu, which never changed. The specialty was biscuits, cornbread, boiled eggs, and occasional barbecue. He'd never tried the barbecue because he had eaten the best in Tuscaloosa at "Dreamland," and he wouldn't partake of that delicacy from any place except there. Before he died, he would return to that "Taj Mahal" for planks of ribs and a sandwich or two of pulled pork.

He entered looking terrible, so after he sat down, she placed a cup of coffee in front of him. He looked up at her with his bloodshot eyes and vile aroma, and she went back to her office, mixed a Bloody Mary, and placed that in front of him as well. He consumed both drinks and muttered, "Biscuit and sausage." Alice was a tall black woman with an infectious laugh, which she emitted the moment he set the empty glass that had contained the vodka mixture down on the counter.

"Brother, did yo' gal drop yo' white ass for you chasin' that lady vet?"

He just stared at her and said, "Nothing like that. My girl has been killed."

Alice just muttered back, "Sorry, sir."

After his breakfast, he went to mass. We need a Catholic church here, he thought. The drive helped him. Upon returning to his area, he found Roman Pascal placing rock in front of his new home, one that he'd never share with Gail. Ramon, unaware of Tony's phone call to Mississippi, began with his super personality. "You know, sir, if we make this entrance in the back the same as the front and erect a dome instead of a perched roof, we'd have the same look as Monticello."

Tony looked at the structure again and, for the first time, realized the stone was white. He had to agree. It was 110 feet long by whatever, and a dome. Now wasn't the time to change the construction except, instead of a flat or peaked roof, make it a large dome. The walls had been erected and portioned back and front. The "beginning" had come up. He was using antique, huge windows, which could be changed if needed. A pseudo perhaps—anything could become a facsimile. He pulled up the complete dimensions from his PC for all the measurements of Monticello. There were fourteen rooms, 110 feet long, 87.9 feet wide, 44.7 feet high, and domed in glass.

"Hey, Ramon, take a break and join me over here, and let's talk."

"Yes, sir, will be there presently," said Ramon. He completed his task and sat down in one of the canvas chairs. Tony served him a beer from the cooler and opened the dialogue.

The first item he mentioned was the dimensions, to learn how close they were to the existing plans. Ramon jumped in immediately, saying, "Monticello sits on a crest over 800 feet. Your structure, already cement-poured, is on a flat river-banked sand area. How would you justify the heavy stone walls, porches, and that dome? My God, even though it is mostly glass, the weight would be horrendous. No, I can't build such a monument."

"No one has asked you to do that," said Tony.

"Just listen to me on this factor. Then have your boss come here, and who knows, a drawing place could be erected. I would want the other homes to be picturesque. That will add to the dimensions of the city."

"I agree, sir, and while we are on the subject, the land east of this house also belongs to me, I'm told. I'm going into Huntsville, the county seat of Madison County, to learn who owns all the property located within the city limits of Cripple Creek," said Tony.

"I have a feeling you will keep me busy building something for a long time," said Pascal.

"That could be correct, but I'm thinking I need you for more white-collar instead of blue-collar work," smiled Tony.

"Sorry, sir, but I wanted to do artistic pursuits when I retired. Keep in mind, I was once a college professor and felt a lot of stress then and swore off any more inside professions," said Pascal.

"I've heard that, but I have a city to build and maintain, and I need experienced help. In addition to experience, I need someone with good common sense. I need someone artistic. I need someone who can be on the job here one day and the next with me on an airplane en route to meet with prospects to move their business and home to Cripple Creek. Who does that sound like?"

"I am happy with my job now. How do you think Ms. Sands will react to my move?" asked Pasquel

"Mad as hell!" said Tony.

"Exactly," replied Pasquel

"Let's look at it another way. What if I were a partner with her in some way, and she entered a request for you to assist me in a business venture with her blessing? Would you hibernate your artistic pursuits and feelings for a bit?" asked Tony.

"Perhaps, but I must know more about your wishes and her pardons." Said Pasquel.

"Understood. Changing the subject for a bit, could you tell me who owns that mountain?" Tony asked, pointing at a peak behind Casey's store.

"Either the federal or state government does."

"Can you find out for me?" asked Tony.

"Probably could, but you could find out in Huntsville at the Judge's office," said Pascal.

"Wanna talk about Monticello again?" asked Tony.

"Yes, but what do you want to do?" asked Pasquel

"Without losing the dimensions we presently have, just adding large porches and a dome that is open—could this be done?" asked Tony.

"Yes, but you have a loan for so much. How will the VA sign off if you make a drastic change without their approval?" asked Pasquel.

"You know a way, though?" said Tony.

"Perhaps, but again, I would need Ms. Sands' involvement," answered Pasquel

"Understood. Now, do you have any more projects lined up after you complete my house?" asked Tony.

"Not really. I'm assuming we will not do anything else along this line until you give and get the project of building riverfront homes along the White River," said Rafel. "By the way, why did you want to know if I had any more projects coming up?"

"Thought we might take a trip to look over some property," answered Tony.

"Just let me know when," puzzled Pasquel.

Chapter 11

Tony slept fitfully on the cot inside the house pier that Sunday night, unsure of what to do next. He planned to pickup Casey to learn the limits of the city. In addition, he intended to call Bill West to find out what procedures must be met before he could take over the mayoral position, but he decided against calling and let the Governor's office handle all the arrangements. He was grief-stricken upon learning of Gail's death and needed some time alone, free from stress.

He made himself a pot of coffee and stretched his legs by walking the distance needed to purchase six plots for riverside houses. He looked at the other side of the river and realized he could build about eight homes there. He would need a bridge, though. He also owned the south side of the county, almost reaching Boston Mountain National Park. Yes, he needed to meet the Governor and arrange enough capital to start this project. The next morning, he went over to Huntsville and secured all the knowledge he needed. He owned most of the eastern part of Madison County, particularly in Cripple Creek Village.

He needed to take a trip to Branson to buy a cell phone and call his stock and bond contacts in Biloxi to assess his wealth. He also needed to phone his attorney to find out what had happened to Gail. He decided to go to Branson tomorrow, but he needed to stay near his phone today in case the Governor's office called. He would contact his attorney while in Branson, and perhaps his attorney could get information regarding his wealth. This morning, he needed to contact Casey and maybe Bill West.

He wondered how "Toby" was doing.

Sitting down with his coffee, he looked across at Casey's store and saw the old teacher walking his way. He poured him a cup of coffee, letting it cool to a drinkable temperature before he arrived.

"Morning, Mr. Gianni, what's new?" said Casey.

"Good morning, Mr. Powers. I just poured you a cup of coffee. How do you feel today?" answered Tony.

"Good, good. Thought we'd browse and look over city limits and ownership," stated Casey.

"I'd welcome that opportunity," said Tony.

"Let me sit and drink my coffee first, then if you don't mind, we can go in your truck," said Casey.

"Of course, take your time," said Tony.

They sat and discussed recent events and what might happen in the future. Tony was surprised that Casey didn't mind him taking the lead in expanding the city and assuming the role of mayor. Casey knew Tony owned a lot of property within the city limits—most of it, in fact—so he was the logical person to take leadership. He appreciated Tony involving him and his son. Their discussion that morning reinforced his dream of abundant living for the city.

"Casey, who is the most reliable and knowledgeable real estate person I can speak with about property and what else we would need?" asked Tony.

"That would be Mrs. Sandra Gilbert of Ozark Realty. She's actually my son's boss but allows him to play State Representative on occasion. She'd probably turn all our deals over to Jeff to handle," said Casey.

"Can you get Jeff on the phone before we continue?"

"Sure." He pulled out his cell phone and called their office in Little Rock. After a brief pause, Casey got on the phone with Mrs.

Gilbert, had a frank discussion with her, then turned to Tony and asked, "Could you be free on Wednesday morning here?"

"Yes, at this house, if that would be okay," answered Tony.

"Mrs. Gilbert, that would be fine. Bring my no-good son with you if you dare," laughed Casey.

They drove all over the known city property and located an area Tony wanted to buy for a future country club. He hoped that his land ownership included the southern bank of the White River. If he developed that side, the Governor would be more likely to approve the construction of two bridges. He could negotiate a deal over that.

To his surprise, by the end of the excursion, he learned that the largest landowner was himself. He had been paying a minimal amount in taxes each year since he had won the property in that long-ago poker game. His property extended northwest from White River to the highway. He was also the sole owner on the south side of the river. He could use this land to help build up Cripple Creek and create special home sites along the riverbank. A portion of his northern properties could be used for home development and downtown expansion. Another section would be ideal for a country club. Somewhere in that area, he also wanted to open a real estate office, a stock and bond office, a bank, and a sporting goods store on the north side of the highway. He really needed the highway to become a four-lane road.

Casey's store, Doctor Sanders' veterinary office, a drugstore, and an antique store were all that made up the village's commercial presence. Immediately, he needed a building for a city hall. He also needed a fire department, a law enforcement building, a utility building, a water department, a street department, and a park. Once the city council was sworn in, he would delegate them to contact different denominations to have churches built on the south side of the White River—on his properties.

But his biggest surprise was learning that the mountain behind Casey's store, previously thought to be owned by the federal government, was actually for sale.

He couldn't wait to meet Sandra Gilbert and the Governor. But he was also eager to spend time with Stella Sands and Roman Pascal again. That evening, he phoned all of them, leaving messages to make themselves available to speak with him next week. The exceptions were the Governor and Jeff Powers, who were already handling their matter.

The next day, he drove to Branson and bought two cell phones with new numbers. While there, he also purchased two pistols from a pawn shop. He bought more presentable clothing for his upcoming meetings. That evening, upon returning home, he found a saved message on his landline from Bill West. He also received a message from Doc Sanders stating that Toby was doing fine and could be picked up at any time.

The next morning, before he had even risen, George Barclay phoned, requesting an appointment. They agreed to meet at his house on Friday afternoon to discuss several matters. Tony also received a message instructing him to come to Fayetteville that day to sign home mortgage papers and pick up other bank-related documents.

He left immediately and headed west, wearing jeans and a polo shirt. He made a mental note to have Roman Pascal complete everything except for the flooring in his bathroom, bedroom, and kitchen. He'd then have Lowe's deliver what he'd bought. The remainder of the house would require a fashionable interior decorator, and he'd need to ask Mr. West about a landscape person to start preparing his yard. If this person was commendable, he'd talk to him about other projects.

He arrived early, so he stopped at a truck stop and had a wholesome vegetable plate and chicken. Later, he went into First

Bank and met with West and the bank's attorney, Ms. Aycock. After the signatures were done, he had a one-on-one with Mr. West about two important visitors. One, the Governor, who would land on Tony's back area and, if possible, would like to come to his home for the appointment. He requested that the City Council members attend also in order to cover all bases. He didn't need a festival, but at a later date, he'd return and enjoy one. He wanted to see the advancements made.

West said that a Mr. Paul Rogers, a landscaper, would contact him tonight on the phone. As soon as he heard from Roman Pascal, he'd phone Lowe's. The Governor would not be available until next Saturday. This would give Tony time to have the house developed and assemble the needed first truck of merchandise from Lowe's.

Roman was asked to put wood flooring in the bathroom, kitchen, and dining room. The balance would later be in marble, and Roman would take care of that. The complete domed roof and the remainder of the structure's roof would be addressed at a later time.

Ms. Gilbert welcomed Tony to the area, but she didn't tell him anything he didn't already know. Actually, she was a waste, but she might be handy in the future.

He drove back to Cripple Creek and discovered Roman Pascal working on the house. Tony was excited that the bathroom was completed and hooked up. Roman had earlier gone by Lowe's and bought an oversized hot water heater for the house. Tony paid him immediately for the appliance.

Tony would use the water pipes that had already been placed when he'd had the streets installed and paved upon his initial arrival. Pete had handled that problem at once. Tony told Ramon when the Governor would arrive and hoped he could complete the wood floors in the kitchen and dining room. He would put a meeting table and chairs in the dining room for the signing in as Mayor, and of course, the same for the City Council. Later, he would donate these nice tables and chairs to the city and have them placed in City Hall. Ramon assured him he'd have this room in good condition. He also wanted to know, "Do you want me to ask for you if she could be here for refreshments?"

"Yes, I do. Great idea. Her beauty will enlighten the occasion. As a reminder, it would be appropriate for you to wear either a black or blue suit with a red tie. Get some black shined shoes also," offered Pascal.

"Yes, I'll attend to that soon," said Tony.

"By the way, I found some people who can make your domed roof and the tiles for the rest of the roof. It's going to cost a pretty penny, but upon completion, your home will be a pseudo-Monticello. The folks that will build it are located in Vermont and will erect it when they bring it down. Ms. Sands and I know a lady who is a recognized interior decorator named Sarah Ford. She will phone you tomorrow about coming down from New York to have a look-see and take measurements toward completing the interior. If you noticed, I added extra closets and shelves all over the house. Interior decorators like those things," said Pasquel.

Pasquel had omitted telling Tony that the central heat and air conditioning were hooked up and working. On his own, Tony hooked up the washing machine, but Pascal had already connected the clothes dryer.

George Barclay, the architect, phoned also and asked, "When can I come by for a meeting?"

"I told him to phone you and gave him your number. I think he'll call soon," said Pascal.

"Good, thank you," said Tony.

While he was writing down so many plans, he thought about how wonderful it would be to have a Walmart placed here after they got people moving in and other key factors improving the city. First, he needed to start playing chamber of commerce and go after factories and other businesses that would help finance the city and, more importantly, bring people in at once.

He got in his boat and cruised the river, thinking about industries or shops he could assist in attracting. He needed a planner to organize this. He would also need to begin now making plans to grow this community quickly.

Important to Tony was to add more artistic components to the city — causes — Music had always been a part of his life, as well as Italian painters. Naturally, he could talk to his dad about music since he'd been involved for a long time. He knew what would be the answer, since he'd heard all his life his father saying, "All cities need to have a symphony orchestra — only need about 30 to 35 musicians to complete your needs to have one."

Now, having art was another problem. Perhaps he would need a theme instead, allowing his ignorance to adjust to what was obvious or what was available. He'd phone Sarah Ford, the home decorator, for suggestions. Personally, he liked Italian Renaissance — people like da Vinci, Michelangelo, Titian, Botticelli, and his favorite, Raphael. Ah!!! Yes, Raphael, who did *Madonna in Landscape*, *The Comple Raschen*, *Pope Leo X with card*, and his favorite: *St. George and the Dragon*. Nevertheless, he wanted either a museum/concert hall or to place art in his home since it was going to be a showplace.

But to do this he'd have to be a zealot. He remembered his mother's voice lately describing: a zealot is a person who takes on a cause. Often, the two become synonymous. Maybe now he too was becoming a zealot like Victor Kiam II, who worked hard all his life for other people. Finally, in 1979, he bought the Remington Company when his wife bought him a Remington Electric Shaver as a gift. His ads featured him pitching, "I liked the shaver so much, I bought the company." Hell, that is what zealot means. Guess I am one too.

Chapter 12

George Barclay was visiting his family in Fayetteville and asked if Tony could meet him at a restaurant named "Sir Calet" and gave him directions. His boat ride had opened his senses, and he was beginning to get excited about what was about to happen.

"Sure, George, I'm on my way." On the way out, he took a Polaroid picture of his house and of the river just to show George. On his way over, he phoned Jeff Powers and asked him to find out more about the mountain behind his dad's store. He was so happy he owned a cell phone that he called his attorney, Jacob Hyman, and had a long talk with him. He instructed Jacob to learn all he could about his wealth. Tony gave him the pertinent info regarding his accounts at banks, stockbrokers, and properties and asked him to get the exact wealth factor.

George wasn't someone you could talk to about using properties to make money. He could, Tony quickly surmised, select from his files residences at many costs and see the end of a project. This was what Tony desired.

"The first six houses were chalet-looking, complete with hidden tool sheds, garages, and skillfully shaped patios. The cost factor would be around $150,000, with an opportunity, with today's financing, to reach a $40,000 profit." His prices for so many other sizes, shapes, and styles could aid him in attaining opportunities to invest in more properties throughout his city, profiting Tony around two million dollars, maybe much more. His property on the riverbank was worth sixty thousand per lot, at other sites twenty thousand and up. All of this was on the north side of the river.

On the south side of the river, it would be advisable to build ten riverside homes, but larger than the structures on the other side. The price there would be around half a million. A subdivision should be planned in this vicinity also. "He'd need to do some work on that," he said.

George also wanted to bid on designing the many city structures on a "dare," he said.

After inquiring about George, Tony learned George was Stella Sands' ex-husband. Not that it mattered, but it appeared that at some time they would need to work with each other. Would that be a problem? Tony's problem was he liked both of them, and he didn't want to be in jeopardy. Best he contacted Stella first. She owned a company that would be building most of the homes. That night, he phoned her as if he was giving her his cell phone number, but he wanted more.

"Hi, Tony, what's happening?" said Stella.

"I didn't bargain for so many details when I moved here. But I need to share a few with you about building my first string of houses. Number one, the interior decorator is coming down from New York to design and equip my home, and I'm going on with Roman's recommendation and having the glass dome purchased and delivered as soon as possible.

She should be the person to decorate the remainder of the riverside houses. I met with my architect today, and I like his file homes," said Tony.

"Who is he?" asked Stella.

"George Barclay," said Tony.

"My ex-husband," said Stella.

"Yes, he told me. Is this going to be a problem?" asked Tony.

"Not for me. We didn't divorce due to work problems. He is a genius when it comes to house building or, for that matter, designing any structure. I'm pretty damn good at what I do, and we don't conflict. We get along."

"Glad to hear. By the way, the Governor is coming up Saturday to swear me in as well as the city councilmen. Could you attend this event as my assistant in my home? You know, like a wife—refreshments, picture-taking, etc.?" asked Tony.

"Why, Mr. Gianni, are you proposing marriage to me?" said Stella, laughing.

"No, Stella, but I need your help. Will you?"

"Of course," answered Stella.

"While I have you on the phone, I don't mind sharing something. My fiancée was killed back in my old hometown. Just learned about it when I tried to phone her to ask her to come up here," Tony explained.

"Oh! I'm so sorry, Tony," she said.

"Yeah, me too. She was shot by someone mistaking her. So, no doubt about it, this is my home forever. Nothing left in New York nor Biloxi. So, with nice people like y'all, I'll find happiness again. Thanks for agreeing to come over here when Huckabee arrives."

After he spoke with Stella, he phoned his attorney back.

"Jacob, I need another instance to be terminated. I need you to rent three trucks for each business I have there and hire the existing staff of each outfit to load up the respective business's entire inventory, equipment, and anything remaining. Everything should be put in containers when loading up. Hire three drivers to haul the trucks to West Memphis, Arkansas, and meet me there upon arrival. Those drivers will be sent back in a rental car. You pay all help, drivers, and your fee for this venture out of my Biloxi bank account. Close down the emptied buildings and sell the properties. I'll hire three drivers from where I am to return the trucks to Biloxi. It could be about two weeks before they'll be returned," said Tony.

"A lot of cloak and dagger about closing down three businesses, but you're paying the tab. I'll see that it's done," said Jacob.

"Yes, and I need you to travel to Branson, Missouri, on the tenth of next month to meet me. We have more activity to get started, and I need to have you with me for a few days. Take a flight up here, and once we are finished, you'll be flying back home," said Tony.

"Tony, you realize I'm licensed in Mississippi and Louisiana only?" said Jacob.

"No, I didn't, but that point doesn't matter. What I want you to do in the future will be done in your present office," said Tony.

"Gotta go now to find a place to store the contents you're sending up," said Tony.

Tony then phoned Pete Oats to learn if he had or knew where he could store the contents of the trucks until the buildings to operate three new businesses were built.

Chapter 13

"Tony, yes, I do. Here in Fayetteville, there is a former K-Mart that's available. You could rent it for a few months, or would you want to buy it at a very reduced price?" asked Pete.

"Buy it. I need a storage site anyway. After you buy it, dig me a hole in the middle of the floor to reuse it for something else. I know this is hush-hush, but I have a lot of 'irons in the fire,' and I need some security. I'll get back with you when you cut the deal. I'll give you a check to make the purchase, so come by," said Tony.

In Starkville, Mississippi, an old closed bank was owned by Tony, and in its vaults was a thousand million dollars of gold and silver. Tony needed it in the floor of the closed K-Mart in Fayetteville as soon as possible. He told Pete to furnish three truck drivers to be handy in a few days to make some hauls. Pete said he could oblige.

In the hole, a big room would be opened; it would be one hundred yards long, fifty yards wide, and thirty yards deep. After the contents were placed in the floor, it would be cemented. Pete was instructed to bring in the necessary equipment to make the dig and sealing without anyone knowing about the contents. At this time, his crews were not working, so he got on the ball and rented equipment to configure the floor of the building. He phoned the real estate office that had handled the sale and closed the deal. He ordered the big equipment to do the floor and to dig deeper. He was in Little Rock and called Tony back to make financial arrangements for the rentals. Tony told Pete to send him three drivers of eighteen-wheelers to meet with him in three nights. He would pay these drivers and was responsible for the rigs to keep everything on a level keel.

Tony called Pete back and asked him to buy three Mack tractor trucks and three steel-bottom 53' trailers. He was to tell his drivers to be ready for any movement at any time. When they arrived in Starkville, a video photographer would secretly film the entire mission and would stick with the transport all the way back to Fayetteville. A team of security guards would guard twenty-four hours a day until the hole was dug in the building for safer keeping. The video would be reproduced until a signing-off by a team of stockbrokers and financiers. They had to stipulate, when they signed off, that this load was owned by Tony Gianni. It was worth a billion dollars. The brokers would be allowed to gain this knowledge and sworn to secrecy. Bill West would be advised by the brokers.

Tony deposited his remaining cash and stocks in the Bank of Fayetteville. His reputation was astounding and unbelievable. He was wheeling and dealing, and his next purchase was to buy the mountain standing high above the city of Cripple Creek. Jeff Powers was working on this purchase. Tony wanted to take an expedition on horseback after the sale was complete to make sure two deeds must come to pass on this mountain. He had to see it to recognize what he must do. He wanted in the trail pact: Jeff Powers, George Barclay, Roman Pasaqual, Bill West, and Mike Huckabee. He called Doc Sanders and asked her to find a herd of trail horses, saddles, and tack for the ride up. He wanted Roman to be on the lookout for a personal ranch site for him at the foot of the mountain. Jeff reported back that this would require congress to allow the sale to happen. Tony could not, nor would not, declare its true use, so congress would only get to know it was for timber and a possible skiing resort with artificial snow. Maybe this would increase the sale.

Tony and Pete got the three trucks into action, and Pete got his trailers buried, filled with gold and silver. The contents in the trailers were swapped out in West Memphis into three rental trailers for distribution in Cripple Creek. Pete had rented three tractor trucks and three trailers for the merchandise. Pete's assistant, Homer

Richards, was responsible for bringing those three to Cripple Creek and parking them. Pete and Tony took care of the burial and brought the newly purchased Mack trucks to Cripple Creek for parking. The other three tractor-trucks were driven to West Memphis two days later.

On the next Saturday, a helicopter landed on Tony's future patio and released the Governor and a few of his people to witness the appointment of Tony as Mayor and his swearing-in of the three city council members. Tony and the Governor seemed to become friends from the very beginning. Admiration and respect prevailed throughout the day, except for the association of Stella and George.

"Tony, here is my private phone number. As you progress in all you do here, keep me informed. I'll have my people compile money in order to build the buildings you'll need to operate. Strangely, we have budgets already there to aid small towns in building necessary structures. I'll have our Commissioner of Roads and Highways call you next week so that we may open up streets and change this highway into a four-lane. The Utility Commissioner will be in touch also. They have a budget to get you going at once with what you'll need. Do you have anything going toward opening factories here?" asked the Governor.

"Yes, I do. I have a friend who will open a plant to build kayaks and canoes, hiring about one hundred people. I'll open five stores. Up first, we'll have six homes built on the White River near my house. Speaking of my house, I'm having it changed so that it looks like Monticello. At the front end will be a garden/patio, and where the paved road divides the properties, I'm donating that land to the city so that we can build a park there. I'm thinking about a fountain there, plus a community center with bleachers for festivals, etc."

"Are you sure there is nothing else I can do for you?"

"Yes, I need churches, schools, and a medical clinic."

"Consider it done, Mr. Mayor," said the Governor.

Huckabee returned to the remainder of the councilmen and women and pressed flesh. Tony talked to Norman and Stella about getting the six houses started as soon as possible. According to them, they would begin tomorrow by developing the landscape and digging septic tank holes.

Paul Rogers, a landscape specialist, called him on Sunday to ask for an appointment for next week to learn about Tony's personal wants and needs. He also wanted to bid on the city's needs and expectations. Tony told him to arrive on Monday twilight for his personal meeting and to bring samples of plants for the city bid.

Governor Huckabee's streets and paving man, Nigel Naples, was excited about this opportunity since the Governor phoned him personally to get this job done right. Other than Pete Oats, no one else except those Tony allowed knew what was buried in the three trailers under the floor of the old K-Mart building. Tony was the sole owner of that building. Today, the flooring would be poured, the guards would diminish, and the sealing of the doors, walls, and roof would begin.

Bill West was due to phone him today for other reasons, but he wanted to talk to him about his purchasing Cripple Creek Mountain. Since he needed to bury vaults in the mountain, he needed West to assist him in buying the vaults. The crews working on the old K-Mart were from Texas and had a lot of experience and proficiency. Nevertheless, the bounty there exceeded more value than only a few people in this land knew about. His own government could put him away, confiscate the precious metals, and place the total amount in Fort Knox, he thought. Naturally, he worried. He had acquired this vast amount in a series of eight poker games he had won on a ship in the Caribbean. He won the ship as well and hired a non-descript Navy to bring it to New Orleans. There, in the darkest of nights, he removed his winnings to a shelter in Starkville, Mississippi.

The underworld wanted this unheard-of gold and silver, but only Tony Gianni knew where it was hidden. If they killed him, they would never know how to steal this precious booty. They would need to figure out another way of discovering its location. He had pledged for years that he knew nothing of its existence. However, he felt the murder of Gail wasn't part of this mystery. Her death had to do with being in the wrong place at the wrong time, and the executioner thought it was Tony driving the Lincoln. He was supposed to die due to getting a capo's daughter pregnant.

Nigel Naples phoned again and stated he would be there on Wednesday afternoon with a team of experts to begin the process of laying out the streets and four lanes of the highway. Tony agreed. Upon hanging up on Nigel's call, his phone rang again. This time, it was General Ambrose McCall of the Corps of Engineers (formerly with the 25th Combat).

"Sir, I served under you in Vietnam," said an excited Tony Gianni. "I helped in surveying the roads to Cambodia."

"The hell you say, and now you are a Mayor?" stated the General.

"That's correct, sir. First day on the job. It's a pleasure to talk to you, sir. What can I do for you?" said Tony.

"No, Mr. Mayor, it's what I can do for you and your city."

"I'm thinking you are addressing the problem we have where the stream is covered up with roots and rubbish, and I need it cleared up and dredged, sir. We are promoting fly fishing, and the river is far from appropriate. Your help would be appreciated, sir."

"Mayor, I'm stationed at Fort Leonard Wood and must make on-site appearances occasionally. I wonder if I could come down to meet with you and look over the White River?"

"That would be great, and while you are here, I'd like you to join a group of advisors as we explore a local mountain that we are considering buying and converting into a tourist attraction."

"Mayor, I would be delighted to join one of my old 'Nam soldiers on this type of sojourn," said the General.

"Great. Does your schedule have an opening on the first Monday of next month?" asked Tony.

"Let me see, Mayor… (a pause) Yes. Willco. Explain how to get there by car."

Tony gave directions and told him he'd stay in his house during his visit. That evening, he decided to hire a secretary and buy a mobile office for a temporary city hall. He needed a liaison to handle the incoming calls he was receiving. He decided to use this number as the mayor's office and use his two cell phones for operational communication. He called Casey for some help.

"Casey, it's Mayor Gianni. I need to hire someone as my secretary. Incoming phone calls are taking over. Do you know someone I can hire to fill that role?"

"The only person I know who could fit that bill would be Stella Sands' sister. Call Stella and ask her if she agrees. I think this woman has been seeking a job," said Casey.

"Thanks. I'll do that now," said Tony.

He phoned her right away. "Ms. Sands, Tony Gianni here. I have a question for you. Is your sister looking for a job?"

"Yes, but why are you asking?"Stella asked.

"I need a secretary, and Casey Powers mentioned her. What do you think?" asked Tony.

"Well, she is qualified, I guess, but I'd rather you talk to her," said Stella.

"How may I contact her?" asked Tony.

"She is in town. Let me try to contact her and give her your number so that the two of you can arrange an appointment."

"Good idea. Please do that. By the way, what is her name?" asked Tony.

"Samantha, but everybody calls her Sam," she said and hung up. So did Tony.

Thirty minutes later, while he was eating lunch at home, Samantha Kimbrough phoned him.

"Mr. Mayor, what can I do for you?" Sam asked.

"Would it be an imposition for you to drive to Cripple Creek so we can discuss the possibility of you being my secretary?" asked Tony.

"When, sir?" she asked.

"Tomorrow morning around ten a.m.," said Tony.

"I'll be there, but exactly where?"

"For the time being, I'm working out of my home. The state will be building a city hall soon, but this is the only structure in town that meets my needs. Ask your sister how to get here. Thank you for returning my message. I look forward to interviewing you. Make up your own résumé if you think that would be appropriate."

"Yes, sir, will do. See you tomorrow. I have a request, though."

"What's that?" Tony asked.

"Don't make coffee. Let me," she said.

Just as he hung up, Sarah Ford called him for an appointment as well.

"Sarah, come at any time. I'm working out of my home until City Hall is built. We'll take care of your needs when you arrive," said Tony.

He phoned Jacob Hymen to get the ball rolling on purchasing the mountain and an extra two miles surrounding the base. Jacob, being extremely conservative, asked why he needed this and what he was going to do about the place in Starkville.

Tony answered short and sweet. "Buy the mountain and sell in Starkville."

He got a call from the architect of the state inquiring about designs for City Hall, the fire department, the police department, and the placement of utilities. The utility department would be in the same building as Mayor's office. He asked this state official how to go about opening a library. It was then that he mentioned he had a bookstore in a trailer and wanted to move it to an appropriate place, like a library.

The person on the other end mentioned that his aunt was a librarian and was seeking a job. Tony told him to have her phone him at this number and, if possible, to get the library construction scheduled second to Mayor's Office. It was mentioned that the fire department would require unique construction due to the services provided to the public from there. His water department chief should be a part of these decisions. Likewise, the same applied to the Police Chief—cells and other important rooms would require the Chief's input.

Tony mentioned that the city had a lot of land to build just about anything, from a place for fly fishing to rodeos, water sports, or maybe even a zoo. The guy on the other end was stunned. He had never heard of a Mayor or anyone else tout their hometown as this guy, Gianni, did. Was he sincere or just "blowing smoke"? By the next day, this man, Stan Robinson, a Black man, had the strongest desire to get acquainted with Tony Gianni. He felt, "Tony is a tornado, but there's always a possibility of getting killed. He is that powerful. He can make you or break you. He is also one of the richest men in America," according to his mentor and uncle, Jack Robinson.

He phoned George Barclay about some plans for two-bedroom cottages that could be located just east of where he had planned a golf course and country club. He had a lot of work for Pete Oats, so he would need another building company to come into the picture. He wanted three new houses built for employees of the city. One would be for his secretary because it would be imperative that she live within the city limits of Cripple Creek.

George understood all of that, and early the next morning, he said he would deliver his drawings and blueprints for the cottages. He would also leave drawings and blueprints for the first six chalets on the riverbank. Each one was somewhat different, but the two-bedroom ones were identical. George was told he was wanted on the horseback journey on the first Monday of next month. He agreed to be there and would video the excursion.

Chapter 14

"Did you talk with Mr. Gianni today?" asked Stella.

"Yes, I did. He mentioned he was looking for a secretary for the city and wanted me to meet him in the morning at ten for an interview. I agreed to do so," said Samantha.

"Well, that's something, don't you think?" said Stella.

"What should I wear?" asked Samantha.

"A navy blue or gray dress. Not a pantsuit. If you don't have one, look in my closet. I'm sure there is something you would like."

"He didn't quote any salary. If he asks, what should I say?" said Samantha.

"Do you want this type of job, or are you satisfied as a bank teller?" asked Stella.

"He said a new building was to be built very soon, and that's exciting. But, sister, that is a long way to drive each day. Is there any place to rent over there?" asked Samantha.

"No, but don't sell this guy short. He is wealthy and believes in doing the best for people around him. He had Jeff Powers inquire in other towns to find out the salaries of all positions connected to his city. He doesn't wait around too long, so if he offers you a job, you'd better take it if you want it because he won't ask a second time," said Stella.

"You know, Stella, he is a good-looking guy, you say, and I'm impressed with him already. Wish I had obtained my degree, but I bet that doesn't matter in this job," said Samantha.

"Get some rest tonight and be bright-eyed when you meet him at his house. Bet that place will be fabulous when completed, with the roof finished and furnished with antiques. Is that where you'll be interviewed?" Stella asked.

"Yes, you said you could tell me how to get there," spoke Samantha.

"It's opposite Casey's Store. Shouldn't be hard for you to find. How are you going to wear your hair?" Stella asked.

"Up and fashionable," said Samantha.

It was a cool autumn morning as Tony took Toby on a brisk riverbank walk. The breeze was welcomed, and the sky, even though blue in spots, was overcast. He left the record player running, and the beautiful tenor of Jerry Vale could be heard as he sang *Al Di La* in the mother tongue.

He went to his truck and drove over to Casey's to have Alice fix him a plate of sausage, three over-light eggs, potatoes, and biscuits. He'd already had a pot of coffee, so he asked for orange juice. His thoughts went to the conversation with General McCall and his future visit to this small town. He figured only the house and the mountain would impress a three-star general. He recalled the general would be nearly seventy now, and the recollection reminded him that the general, a West Pointer, was tops in his engineering studies.

Without revealing anything, he'd try to pick his mind about the best use of a mountain.

He went back home and cleaned the kitchen and bathroom. He placed the drawings flat on the table for her to visualize. If she didn't work out, he'd advertise in the *Fayetteville* newspapers, but he dreaded doing that. A lot of riff-raff comes through your door. If she did accept, he'd let her spend the night in his home while he took a trip to Fayetteville to shop at Wal-Mart.

He phoned Pete Oats and asked him to stop by before he got busy.

He stood up and walked through the house just to get a feeling of home when someone knocked on the back door. He thought it was Samantha, but when he opened the door, it was a stranger from Fayetteville. He'd never seen this man of about sixty.

"Mr. Gianni, I'm Todd Nixon, your part-time druggist and city councilman," he said, grinning.

"Well, Todd, I'm very happy to meet you at last. Come on in," said Tony.

Todd looked over the drawings and commented on how pretty they were.

Tony was glad to hear someone else appreciate this version of how the houses looked.

"Mr. Mayor, if you use this type of constructed house, and I assume local construction companies will be used in the building, then you are on your way to building a great-looking city," said Nixon.

"I'm covered up with details on all of this, so I'm hiring a secretary to assist me until we move into a city hall we have planned. Leave me your phone number, and when I get it all together, we'll have a city council meeting. I'm expecting a prospective secretary candidate at any moment."

Todd stood, shook hands, and said he was leaving.

"I am so pleased to be working with you on this great idea of building a city and having someone of your caliber to run it," said Nixon.

She knocked on the door first and then walked in with her brown hair pulled up and wearing a dark blue suit. She was awesome, thought Tony.

"Good morning, sir. I'm Samantha Sands. May I make you a pot of coffee?"

Tony just nodded and took in her body with its many curves and movements.

"How do you like your coffee?" she asked.

"Black with two spoons of Splenda, not sugar," answered Tony.

"Well, Samantha, tell me about yourself. But first, let me ask a few questions," said Tony.

"Of course, but may I ask you a question first?" she said.

"What is it?" asked Tony.

"What exactly are you seeking in a secretary?" she asked.

"Someone who is devoted, can handle my schedule, and is acquainted with all schedules from each department of the city. Someone aware at all times of what, who, when, and where I can better serve the residents of this city. Computer proficient. Someone who, later, can manage other employees of this office. To never share any information unless I have given permission to do so. Must live here in this city. Work with, and not for, the councilmen and women. Work long hours for city hall but longer for the citizens. Dress as you do now and not be a showpiece."

To enjoy and appreciate your job. I am not a severe taskmaster but expect the best from you at all times.

"Sir, I don't understand the requirement of living here when there is no place to reside, rent, or even camp out," she said with a smile.

He grinned as he explained, "I am building a house for you to live in as soon as possible. In the meantime, you'll reside in this house, and I shall live in my pier house. In addition, I'll supplement your salary with a city automobile. Fuel furnished. You'll need this for the many tasks you must do in Fayetteville and at the county seat. I'm tempted to send whoever is selected for this job to another city that our Governor selects for a three-day session on what is required for the Mayor/City Secretary role.

"Upon returning, you'll be very busy for at least a month designing how we should administratively run a city. Some of what you'll learn will be tossed away, some will be kept and expanded. Maybe by the time you return, your house will be built, and you can move in. Your salary will be two hundred a week plus a bonus that I will pay, not the city. You will have medical and life insurance. As a matter of fact, when you return, fill this house with insurance agents placing their bids for city business. After you achieve this, we will sit with the city council and decide what we will be able to pay, assuming our population will reach a certain amount within a year. I'll give you the number of vehicles we'll take care of in the first year for you to buy. For now, use a purchase order method, and on that form, indicate all three prices.

"Now, without any more discussion from me, please tell me your job experiences and education. I'm assuming you are not married based on your introduction, where you mentioned your last name being the same as your sister's."

"Yes, our grandfather was Tommy Sands, and our father was Rick Sands. Both were singers. My sister and I each attended Vanderbilt University in Nashville. She graduated, but I still need another year. I majored in Finance; she majored in Business. I work as a bank teller—boring, but I meet a lot of nice people. Yes, I know how to use computers to a certain degree. I admit that when people sell us at City a way of communication, they will be obligated to teach us how to use this form of doing business. Perhaps the folks that sell bank systems would be adept at setting up a system for city business, including utilities, telephones, and PC work. I've worked while in college at a tire dealership as an accountant assistant, worked as a cashier at a department store, and, for a short time, worked as a clerk in a hospital," explained Samantha.

"Our city council would be upset if I didn't interview other prospects, so I must ask you something that won't be in the notes when I propose hiring an assistant," said Tony.

"Yes, sir, what is it?" she asked.

"I have many personal secrets and have been in many secret battlefields. I suspect I'll be in more, so my question is this: Will you have my back, and can I trust you?"

She paused for a while and finally said, "If it isn't illegal, and will you have my back if I should accidentally become involved?"

"Is that a yes?" he asked.

"Yes, since you just told me I could count on you also," said Samantha.

He stood up, slightly bowed at her, and said, "I'll make my decision on who I'll recommend by the end of the week."

She departed, and he made a mental note to connect with a Ford dealer to start buying vehicles for the city. But first, he needed to get state assistance in hiring a utility director, water director, fire chief, police chief, and personnel director.

He received a phone call from Pat Howard for a job interview, which he set up for tomorrow morning. He also phoned a friend of Pete Oats based on Pete's recommendation for an interview on Friday. He called for a council meeting on Saturday morning at his house to discuss several matters. The Ford dealer's sales manager said he'd bring two SUV Ford Broncos over for the Mayor and City Manager. Tony said fine, as long as he could prove the price matched those of other municipalities. Both were pearl white and equipped as four-wheelers. Now he would have proper transportation instead of an old pickup truck. Not to worry, though, he thought. I'll always keep that truck. Toby enjoys sleeping in it, and I think I'm cool driving it. As a matter of fact, he felt older men should all drive pickups and have a dog to take to the woods or water to enjoy what God has given them.

Nigel Naples had begun bringing his paving vehicles into town. He walked over from his truck to greet them. "Nigel, George Barclay has told you—or should I ask, has given you—plans to do this project?"

"Yes, sir, he has. He told me the state would partner with y'all in paying for our work. Mr. West at the bank said, credit-wise, it would be okay. Says you could buy about anything you want, including a city," said Nigel.

"Well, son, it's this way. Give me your tab when you complete your job. I'll call the Governor and get his share, and I'll pay the city's share. When the city begins collecting taxes, they'll pay me what they owe.

"So don't worry, you'll get your pay. Now, in doing this, you'll be doing curbing, sidewalks, and parking lots. If you follow George's plans, two of the streets will need a slight lift as you approach the river. According to George, this area is for future bridges. Next month, when you begin paving on the south side, come by to see me first. I need to put a park near the areas marked for schools. When all is completed here, see me again about the area just north of the city. I haven't bought it yet, but it will be very important and profitable for you. By the way, where do you live?"

"In Fayetteville. Not married. Have an apartment," he muttered.

"You need to move here to one of the places we'll be building," said Tony.

"Maybe I'll do that and have my entire operation moved over here. People who work for me would like that," said Nigel, the middle-aged bachelor. That evening, he called George Barclay, another bachelor, and bounced ideas with him. They agreed to select some empty area east of the city and propose it as an ideal location for a commercial business district to generate quick revenue for the city. It was understood that before Tony could approach investors to open factories here, a workforce needed to be assembled. He told George he'd start working on it immediately.

He called Roman Pascal to find out if subcontracting could be done immediately for constructing an assortment of buildings in a proposed industrial park. The only way was to bring in a construction company to build metal buildings for plants, storage, schools, and churches. Roman told him his roof would arrive this Sunday, and after a night's sleep, the crew would begin Monday morning, erecting it in the properly marked area. It would be bolted down precisely, and necessary vehicles would be brought in from Little Rock to do this. "They are coming up now and will arrive on Sunday. Best you get out of the way and stay in your selected City Hall for at least a week," said Roman.

"Very well. Bought a mobile office that will be here on Monday," said Tony.

Both laughed, and with Toby loaded in the pickup, they went to Casey's Store for the announcement.

Grading crews arrived with their equipment to prepare sites for City Hall, the library, the police department, the fire department, utilities, the water department, and the entire industrial park. This was the initial grading phase to build the city of Cripple Creek. Roman would also grade for six new homes and the entire section of the city designated for future housing development.

Chapter 15

He used his cell phone that evening and asked Samuel Sonheim in Biloxi to give him a rundown on the money he'd made using his firm.

"Tony, where the hell are you? Been trying to run you down! Wild, man, absolutely wild. The market has tripled your stocks, and if you ever go public with any of your investments you keep hidden, please call me. We'll make a lot of cash. Now, Tony, where—Hello! Hello! Hello! Where are you?"

The next morning, on behalf of Tony's enterprises, Jacob Hymen collected thirty-five million dollars from this account and deposited it into Tony's bank in Fayetteville, Arkansas.

The next day, Tony placed thirty-four million dollars into the City of Cripple Creek's opening account. He would add more when the bank opened an account via a thirty-million-dollar loan. Tony would need to appear at the bank next week to get the ball rolling.

For the building of roads and digging for water springs, vouchers would be submitted by the governor next week as well. The governor signed purchase orders to have sufficient buildings for the City of Cripple Creek next week. The estimates arrived, and they were within the budget requirements.

Now, Tony needed people. The "Chiefs" had not submitted the employment application yet! They needed to be hired immediately to assist in building according to their specifications. He told the governor's assistant that he didn't want to step on anyone's toes, but if he was needed to intercede, they should feel free to call him. He gave the landline number for City Hall and his cell number in case the prospects needed to talk to him privately.

That night, the prospect for Police Chief phoned him while he was eating some of Alice's vegetables. The prospect, along with his family, was driving up from Russellville, Arkansas.

SUNDAY

The crew with the dome had made initial adjustments as they laid the dome down on the walls. The electricians were waiting for completion before they could hook up. His house was in its adjustment period. He'd let Sarah Ford do her magic, and then he would handle the basics.

On Monday, he needed to phone Samantha to learn if she wanted the job. He felt she would accept after he told her about the recent changes.

"Hello," she answered. "Who is this?"

"Samantha, this is Mayor Gianni. May I talk to you at this time?"

"Yes, sir, you may."

"There is a change in the job you inquired about."

"In what respect, sir?"

"Pay has doubled, and so has the position. I need you, if you accept, to be City Manager. I'll hire the other two ladies who applied for your job as secretaries—one for computer operations and one for liaison with department heads. We'll hire more help under you as we see the need. Your new car is here, and I need you to begin work now. Do you want this job? By the way, the house package is still part of your benefits."

"Yes! Let me resign from the bank tomorrow morning, and I'll come your way," said a happy lass named Sam.

"No, do this: Design a job application and business cards for you, Casey Powers (City Councilman), Todd Nixon (City Councilman), Elizabeth Sanders (City Councilwoman), and me. Use this phone number and address on all cards: #1 Cripple Creek Drive, Cripple Creek, Arkansas. Use this area code for the time being. Connect with a sign painter to paint welcome signs for all entrances and exits of this town. The signs should read:

Welcome to Cripple Creek, Arkansas, Fly Fishing Capital of the Ozarks.

Now, come on in and meet with me and Pete Oats about your home."

She giggled, opened her fridge, poured herself a big glass of white wine, and called her sister and then her dad.

Tony phoned Pat and 'Cilla and told them to come to work tomorrow at one o'clock. He left two other females giggling and happy.

The city council on Sunday was full of questions for him to answer. As far as hiring someone, they felt he knew what he wanted, and they had no idea. So, he hired all three.

He called Pete Oats and asked him to come in around one o'clock for a meeting about the two-bedroom housing.

He then called the Secretary of the Interior about the nearby mountain to get the ball rolling on this purchase. The man on the other end, Secretary Bray, mentioned that the Governor of Arkansas had sent a communication about the matter. He was intrigued as to why someone wanted this done until the Mayor explained the specifics about timber, recreation, and storage. He said he'd discuss it with the president and call back after his meeting with President Reagan. He added that he liked the idea but asked what dollar figure Tony could pay. Tony gave him no answer to that.

Finally, he called the Superintendent of Education for Arkansas and went through the same routine as all the other objectives of building a present-day city. He got a very positive response—the superintendent would love to come up and learn more. Tony invited

Dr. Hayes to come at his convenience and schedule. He gave Dr. Hayes Samantha Sands' name and requested that he contact her regarding his visit and schedule.

He got into his new SUV and drove closer to the mountain. As he neared it, he felt that the name "Mount Reagan" would be appropriate. He circled the entire mountain, making mental notes along the way.

Upon returning to his home, three visitors were there: Sarah Ford was browsing each room, while Pete Oats and Samantha Sands sat at the kitchen table, having coffee and studying the two-bedroom house he was about to build for her.

Stella Sands knew Sarah Ford and was staying there until she returned to New York. Pete and Samantha completed their design changes, and he went back to sealing off K-Mart.

Samantha sat down to learn from each other. She had done all he asked and had also stopped by a mobile home lot, ordering an office trailer to be brought to Cripple Creek in three days for use as a temporary city hall. She also told him that while ordering the cards and job applications, she had ordered three Apple computers, one old typewriter, office supplies, and a desk and chair for herself.

The supplier would deliver the items and hold a computer class on Saturday mornings for all employees. They received this on P.O. #1. The car was P.O. #2, the mobile home/office was P.O. #3, the sign company was P.O. #4, the Corps of Engineers was P.O. #5, Pete Oats Construction was P.O. #6, the Fayetteville bank was P.O. #7, truck tags were P.O. #8, car tags were P.O. #9, mobile phones from the Mayor were P.O. #10, and rental to Casey Store was P.O. #11.

She had completed each P.O. and was inquiring about the bank and its involvement with the City of Cripple Creek. Above all, she needed their bank account number and present balance. She intended to be the final authority when it came to the city's banking and its complete connection with Anthony Gianni. She needed to know about all documents related to the city. Tony Gianni had been good to her, and she wanted to return the favor.

First of all, after updating him, she needed to find out what he wanted from her. She had already been asked the question: Tony Gianni is a millionaire; why does he want a city?

She phoned the telephone company and ordered city hall desk phones and two fax machines. She also ordered additional cell phones for the Mayor and, of course, herself—P.O. #12.

Kroger Company had phoned, and she would return that call along with one from Walmart. The electrical workers and their union had also phoned, but the Mayor did not get the message.

Delivery trucks were backed up on the highway, trying to figure out where to unload. Among the trucks was the Mayor's house furniture from New York. The City of Cripple Creek was beginning its growing pains.

YEAR LATER
Chapter 16

Within a year, Tony Gianni's city began taking shape. The downtown buildings were now housing businesses and folks interested in the empty buildings, waiting on correct rental from Cripple Creek Realty, owned by Tony and Stella Sands. On the highway was a Dairy Queen store, McDonald's, and room for plenty more fast food or quick-service-type businesses. The city's important structures were erected, like the police department, fire department and station, utilities, two banks, the water department, and four cafes. All were within reach near downtown, but among these buildings was City Hall, the only high-rise building so far.

The streets were laid out, and a vast number were paved. Pete Oats Company built twenty three-bedroom, low-cost houses in an area known as Central Park, now sold and occupied. Sixteen two-bedroom houses were in an area known as Sands, and they were occupied. Pete rented six, plus Samantha's, which the city owned, and the balance was sold. The six places in the Riverbank area were completed and sold. It was known as Riverbank Place North. Stella then went to the other bank to build another subdivision that would be known as Riverbank Place South.

The state of Arkansas entered the picture and built, in a designated area, the three schools that were needed. While waiting for the construction to be completed, students attended classes the first year in pre-fab mobile units located near downtown. Tony's number-one pride in construction was the sports fields built on the south side. He had an area he'd designated for the construction of a medical clinic. Baptist, Methodist, and Assembly of God congregations had started building their buildings on land donated by the city. The Catholic congregation was meeting weekly in an empty building downtown and was planning on building a cathedral closer to the downtown area that would be huge and majestic.

Tony wasn't resigned to allow Samantha to do his job as mayor, but his day was filled with appointments and meetings. He had luncheons with political folks from the state and nation, asking the same questions: Where did you get your money? Who are you? What is the future here? Newspapers and television were worse; they were too personal. His evenings were spent home alone, except with Toby, just to be out of the spotlight. Wednesday nights were nicer since that was the city council meeting night. Each councilperson had a long agenda and was allowed thirty minutes to present and receive information of some type to and from the mayor. At the end of individual meetings, the mayor allowed his time to discuss actions he'd been involved with. After that, the council voted.

Sarah Ford had done an excellent job designing and using common sense with his home. Actually, he used only his bedroom, kitchen, and bathroom. The remaining rooms were showpieces. They met in his office at home. It was large enough for that and a small party if needed. His office staff, chiefs of police and fire departments, and councilpersons all attended his Christmas party. He gave all these people wristwatches for Christmas presents. They gave him mountain climbing equipment plus an announcement they had hidden from him: A person he wanted to hire as city accountant director, who had previously turned him down, changed his mind and had come on board. He was Ken Antoinilli, an Italian from Bismarck, North Dakota. He had a large family and, of course, was Catholic. Tony was told he even enjoyed Samantha's PO system.

Now that the city had taken on a life of its own, Tony could concentrate on the mountain. Finding personnel to fill positions had been a problem. Police were the hardest. He reflected on how he had a chief but no one else, so he contacted the police academy and asked for help. It happened to be graduation time, and many good men were looking for jobs. They couldn't believe a city existed that had no crime. To them, at first, it was Mayberry, and they thought the mayor and chief just wanted "Barney." After acceptance and making an immediate move to a place almost like "Camelot," no one wanted to leave. When they arrived, all preparations had been made, from exact sizes for uniforms to fitted patrol cars. The Ford dealer and sign painter did as directed. The autos were all four-wheel drive with powered-up motors. All they needed were experienced officers to lead them. The chief took care of that problem by offering positions to retired officers from all states. He filled those positions and brought in experienced cops who truly thought this was utopia. These same "retirees" helped in bringing in firemen the same way. Tony had brought in the Fayetteville chief for a week to help design police headquarters and the jail. No one knew how expensive this undertaking was except the designer.

"Mr. Mayor," he said, "crime does pay. Our justice system requires more and more daily. Sir, have you made room and hired people for your courtroom?"

In all this designing and building of a city, he'd forgotten something as important as a courthouse and a judge. He called his friend and attorney, Jacob Hyman, and explained what he'd done.

"Tony, there are times I feel you are the smartest man I've ever known, but you can do things occasionally that make me think you are a real dumb ass. This is now one of them. Build the courthouse next door to your police station. Have entranceways connected. Call your state supreme court and have them send you a judge. Plead innocence of your stupidity and thank them profusely."

The state of Arkansas built all utilities, water, and telephone services and even participated in constructing the pole lights, a new thing called LED lights, which gave a glow that, coupled with the new emerald green grass and the concrete-paved roads, made this place unforgettable. As a matter of fact, the street that brought shoppers into downtown was named "Unforgettable Way."

Tony loved this place immensely, but he retained a desire to always make it better. Samantha, the second most powerful person in Cripple Creek, convinced the city council to erect a six-foot statue of Tony and place it on the lawn of City Hall on the city's first day, November 18, 1989. It was now 1990, and the anguish of the buried treasure in an old K-Mart building was giving him nightmares. He had to go through with a plan he had begun formulating a year ago and place it in the mountain. The statue was being built.

Even Samantha didn't know the real reason he wanted to buy the mountain. She'd been told he wanted the cedar timber, to build many chalets on the sides of the beautiful mountain, a year-round artificial snow ski slope, a four-side zip line, and rodeo grounds at the base of the mountain. But why did he need eight garbage dumpsters in connection with this mountain? He just told her it was none of her or anyone else's business.

The harder he pushed, the more obstinate the Department of the Interior became. One evident clue was that they were controlled by the Republican Party, which wanted to name a mountain somewhere "Mt. Ronald Reagan."

"Well, hell, we'll name this mountain Mt. Ronald Reagan. It will stand over our city."

"No," was still the answer.

At the base of the mountain was an area suitable for building a concert hall plus parking. On the other side was enough space to build a rodeo arena plus parking, animal structures, and an elaborate, mobile bleacher setup. It was extremely unique if Tony could find someone who shared his vision.

He was proud that the schools were being built, and he had contacted a person in California experienced in handling everything related to building stadiums, gymnasiums, and basketball courts. They had agreed that if the state took care of erecting the buildings, the city would pay for the football, soccer, softball, baseball, tennis courts, basketball courts, and strength-conditioning buildings. At a later time, if the need arose, an aquatic center would be added.

Eventually, tax money would come in, and Tony's estate would expand. However, he needed to contact Bill West for stock sales and splits to be placed in the city of Cripple Creek's bank account. The city needed to buy another fire truck and expand the water department's fire plugs throughout the city.

Tony had been successful in bringing jobs to the area through three large manufacturers: Ozark Kayak–Pontoon–Sailboat MFG, hiring three hundred; AYASTIGI Motor Company, owned by the Japanese, hiring two thousand and building small pickup trucks; and Adams Tire, a plant that hired two hundred and manufactured heavy equipment and tractor tires. That totaled thirty-five hundred jobs in the industrial park, with more businesses inquiring about placing their investments in the U.S.A. If the trucks "took off" in sales, then more opportunities would arise, bringing success and money to the city.

"Boss, I must ask you this simple question: have you considered making a move toward a golf course?" asked Samantha.

"Yes, some men in the Exchange Club have mentioned building a country club," said Tony.

"Well, what's the answer here?" asked Samantha.

"We'll need two courses—one for the country club and one named Cripple Creek Municipal Course—but land isn't available for both. We must consider having sufficient housing for the future. Not everybody has the money to buy a home, so as mayor, I must help them have a place to live. A housing authority will have to open with an apartment complex. So, ask the men who want to have a country club to come in for a meeting with you, Ken, the council members, and me," said Tony.

"What if they have changed their minds and a country club would not sustain itself?" she asked.

"Same option—we must build apartments first and rent them out from the city," he said.

"Okay, tell me the names, and I'll assemble them for the meeting. Should I ask them from the start where their money is coming from?" she inquired.

"No, I'll do that at the meeting in some form or another," he said.

"You once mentioned building an arena for rodeos and ranch activities. Are you still in that mindset?" she asked.

"I am, and I will be if the sale of the mountain is consummated," he said.

"Why?" she asked.

"It will bring in tourists, stores, cafés, and other businesses that could grow with their participation. This would also give us a sales tool to attract motels to build here. All we have is one hotel, and it is downtown. We need at least three on the strip. As you know, this is where the fast-food companies are most likely to build," he said.

"You haven't taken any time off this year. Are you planning on taking some time and vacationing somewhere?" she asked.

"I live in the best vacation area in this part of Arkansas. I can fly fish at any time. I want to attend events in our concert hall, play some golf in this town, put on a ten-gallon hat and watch a rodeo in my hometown, go zip-lining from a mountain, ski from a mountainside in my hometown, take my boat out for any water sport in my hometown, and soon step out of my office, cross the street, and enter a shooting gallery—right here in my hometown. Any more questions?" he said.

"No, but I'd love to have a grist mill restaurant on the White River. And I am in love with you, but so are a lot of other people. Will you marry me?"

"Yes. I love the idea of a grist mill on the river. I'd also like to place a Ferris wheel and other amusement park rides somewhere in town.

Now, about the love business—you respect and admire what I do, and I'm flattered that you and other people say you love me. But, Sam, I've been in many strange battlefields in my life. I loved one woman, and she was killed because she wanted to marry me. It ended sadly. I haven't gotten out of that strange battlefield," he said with a tear in his eye.

She turned and walked away.

Chapter 17

The phone rang, and the call was from Washington, D.C. He answered as he was accustomed to, "Hello, Mayor Gianni here. What may I do for you?"

A deep bass voice stated, "You idiot, you already own the damn mountain you are making such a problem about. Check your county courthouse further." Then he hung up.

Tony gathered his land acquisition records, which covered nearly all of Madison County, and scrutinized them at length. In his estimation, he actually owned the mountain, but he wanted a legal interpretation from a judge or federal government official. He traveled to Huntsville to the county land records office and spoke to a clerk who seemed very knowledgeable. Since he was the mayor, he received the royal treatment from the clerk. She pulled the files, which revealed that the land was owned by a person named Anthony Gianni from Biloxi, Mississippi, who had acquired it from the previous owner, Edgar Emmons of South Africa. The transfer of ownership had occurred on October 2, 1978.

Taxes and other fees had been paid annually from the office of Jacob Hymen of Pascagoula, Mississippi, on behalf of Mr. Anthony Gianni of Biloxi, Mississippi. According to the records, Mr. Gianni owned the majority of the land from Boston Mountains National Park almost to the Missouri border and as far west as Washington County. This land was marked. Eastward, it stretched from Washington County to ten miles past Cripple Creek Village. All land north was owned by Mr. Gianni, except for homesteads and municipal properties north of Madison County.

Tony summoned the probate judge for confirmation. Judge Hill appeared, having heard of Tony, and was glad to be of assistance. After carefully reviewing all maps, letters, and payment records, he confirmed that Mr. Gianni was the sole owner. Tony thanked him and handed him an envelope containing $500 in cash. The judge had written and signed a letter verifying this matter.

Tony felt like he had just escaped another strange battlefield. He got back in his car and returned to Cripple Creek. Once he had passed the Huntsville city limits, he "whooped" and "hollered" all the way home.

The next morning, he called an emergency city council meeting at his office downtown. He arrived early and had four copies of the judge's letter ready for distribution to the council. The three council members arrived on time but were not in the best of moods. Tony reached into his bottom desk drawer, pulled out a bottle of Jack Daniel's, and poured each councilperson a shot. His own glass was already poured, and he was gleaming at it.

"I hereby call this emergency meeting to order on December 2, 1990," said the mayor.

"What's the emergency, and why are you pouring whiskey?" asked Elizabeth.

"Doctor, I learned this morning who owns the mountain," said the mayor.

She looked at the whiskey in her glass, then at her two fellow council members, and asked, "Who?"

Tony slipped copies of the probate judge's letter to each person and said, "Read."

In unison, they looked up at Tony and said, "How did you do that?"

"If you drink all that I have given you and believe what I tell you is true, I'll explain everything. But what I say stays here. I do have a request, though—could Samantha meet with us and hear what I have to say?"

All three nodded yes.

He summoned a surprised Samantha into his office. He began telling his story, starting with the poker game on the cruise liner up to this point, though he left out many personal details.

At the conclusion of his story, the four were eager to ask questions. He began with Samantha.

"Mayor, will you continue to build this city?"

"Yes, but it will never be huge—just a wonderful place to live and enjoy," he said.

Casey was next. "What will you do about the mountain?"

"I'll use a small part of it for my personal use. The rest will be for recreation and an opportunity to generate income for the city. I've already indicated some plans—golf courses, bringing in more industry, a grist mill restaurant by the river that offers the best steaks imaginable, a rodeo arena with a western concert stage, chalets built on the mountain, extra housing, a zip line and trolley from top to bottom, an amusement park with a Ferris wheel, a merry-go-round, a putt-putt golf course, a bowling alley, a Parks and Recreation Department, and a complete senior citizens complex.

"All of this will be up to you and our accountant. In time, we'll also need to bring in a personnel and human resources director. Again, all of this will be stressful for Samantha and me, so as time moves on, the City of Cripple Creek will grow bit by bit, and we'll need help," said Tony.

"What will you do about the mountain as far as the city is concerned?" asked Casey.

"Nothing, really. I won't sell it to the city or anyone. However, I'll allow the city to use it in some respects. Believe me, this is an opportunity for all of us. I've been thinking about building chalets as rental properties for the city, a Christmas setting at the very top, and allowing the city to use the zip line and trolley. But timber sales and any mineral rights will remain mine."

"I'm authorizing Pete Oats and Roman Pascal as part-time building agents for the city. They will work on a contract basis. They will be able to either rent or long-term lease certain vehicles to be used on the mountain. This will be city business because the chalets will be owned by the city. Maybe later on, we can establish a Parks and Recreation Department to manage the rentals, oversee the rodeo, and advise us on other activities.

"General Ambrose is headed this way to see about bringing his crews in to work on the river. For now, we need to dredge, remove tree limbs and junk, and open the river wider at our point. I also want to build a pond to increase our fish population.

"Holiday Inn, Ramada Inn, and Marriott Inns have expressed interest in building motels on the strip. Likewise, McDonald's, Taco Bell, Kentucky Fried Chicken, and Burger King want to setup on the strip. McDonald's wants an extra location downtown, designed in a café style rather than the fast-food type on the strip.

"Now, has anyone mentioned interest in building a skating rink?"

Casey spoke up. "Ol' Hank Dixon said he'd like to do that, but he wants it downtown. I told him I'd talk to you about it, but I didn't think downtown would be acceptable."

"No, we have most of that covered in town. Perhaps at the amusement park area, west of town. That's where we'll need to place the Ferris wheel, merry-go-round, etc. We'll probably need to place the arcade there also," said Tony.

"By the way, I'm presenting the three of you with a gift and a treat. To be placed at the amusement park will be 'PALS,' a hot dog kiosk, and you three are the owners. I paid for the franchise. It will be up to you to decide who will manage what," said Tony, laughing.

"I'm too old to cook wieners," said Elizabeth.

"Me too," said Todd.

"Anyway, it belongs to y'all. Let me tell you, they have excellent sandwiches, and you'll make a lot of extra money this way. I'll have them send over a seasoned manager to teach y'all what you need to do."

"Good, I'll need help, I'm sure," said Casey.

"Anything else?" asked Samantha.

"Yes, all of us need to consider senior citizen involvement in our community," said Tony.

"Let them be employees of 'PALS,'" said Todd.

"Damn good idea," said Elizabeth.

On the way out, Casey grabbed Tony by the arm and said, "Tony, we must build a farmers' market. Place it near the industrial park area. I've been thinking about selling out, and I could manage the farmers' market. Shell Oil wants to buy my property and build a super station there. I agreed. We need to have a place for truckers to fill up."

"What about Alice?" asked Tony.

"Give her a place downtown and feature a spot for breakfast that she could manage," said Casey.

"Good idea, Casey, but are you sure this is what you want?" said Tony.

"Guess you wonder what to do about a bait shop?" asked Casey.

"Build one near the bridge going over to the south. If there are restrictions about property values, place it under the bridge," said Casey.

"I'll talk to General Ambrose about this and let him engineer a place that would be appropriate," said Tony.

"You know something, Casey? I think the General would enjoy moving down here. When we went up the mountain, he remarked what a beautiful place this was and how much he hated the heavy traffic in a big city like St. Louis. He said he'd love to own one of the two-bedroom houses. If y'all on the council ever feel like expanding, the General would be a good invite, along with Roman Pascal. That would make five, which seems like the appropriate number. We need a councilperson to live on the south side of the city, and Roman is building a house over there," said Tony.

"Yeah, gotta agree on five, Tony. We need young blood as time goes by. The General isn't young but has an engineering education and savvy; he could be a big asset to the city. I would love to have a young man or woman representing the industrial park region. Sooner or later, we are going to need an airport. We have land on the western side for that. These plants own small aircraft that bring executives from their home offices, and transportation with aircraft for residents is not available. Many residents are pilots and, in time, could buy their own small planes," said Casey.

Tony went home early to be alone for a while. His soul felt morbid and lonely. He fixed a solid dinner of vegetables and pot roast he'd cooked in his crockpot, and the meat was tender and nourishing. That evening, he took three phone calls of very little importance on the city phone but nothing on his cell phone.

He realized all that evening how much he missed Gail. To pass the time, he watched the news, especially the special on how President Reagan had impacted the world lately. He agreed with what most of the commentators said about the President's efforts and successes. He had only a glass of wine with his dinner and then went to bed.

Chapter 18

Three hours later, his city phone began ringing constantly until he answered. It was his Aunt Louise, who said, "Tony, it's your Aunt Louise. How are you?"

"How are you, Auntie?"

"Tony, do you know both of your parents are dead and the studio is in a mess?"

Tony said, "Tell me the part about my parents, please."

"Well, your mother died from a heart attack about a year ago at home. Your dad left us when he entered the nursing home a few months back. He had cancer of the bladder. He passed away in the nursing home out on Long Island. He began trying to find you but couldn't. He gave the studio over to you, and it has been operating with that nasty Thomas LeCroix running things. Now he has gotten the studio in debt and is making a big mess because your dad died and gave the studio to you rather than to him. He called me cussing and thinks he knows where you are. He wants you to come and see him and bring money for his back pay and the debts of the studio. Your dad left Carlos Clemente, his attorney, in charge, but he refuses to do anything until you tell him what to do," she said.

"Do you have this Clemente's phone number?"

"Well, here it is," she said and recited the number. "Tony, where are you? I phoned a man in Biloxi from the phone number I found in your dad's phone book, but he said you didn't live in Biloxi anymore and he didn't know where the hell you were. Now, again, where are you? You're the only kin I have, and I'm living in your parents' place. Is that okay?"

"Yes, Auntie. I'll call Mr. Clemente and get an idea of what the tab is, and I'll send him the money owed. I also want to know where the money earned is located. I'll see you in New York. I'll send someone to get you and bring you to me. Keep quiet about talking to me except to Mr. Clemente. Don't be involved with this LeCroix fellow. I'll handle him. Goodbye, Auntie. I'll see you soon."

He then hung up, grief taking over. His parents were dead. Oh, how he wished he had brought them out here. They had protected him all his life. They had been in danger, and he had been free for a long time. He wept for the balance of the night. Now, he had to correct mistakes made by his family and himself.

The next morning, he called in for work and began the process of making corrections. He phoned Mr. Clemente and discussed how much money was owed. According to Clemente, it totaled nearly $75,000.00. He instructed Mr. Clemente to pay off all debts, especially salaries. He further asked Clemente to tell Mr. LeCroix he'd be there soon and would discuss the future of the "famous" record label and studio.

At that moment, all employees other than LeCroix were dismissed. All contracts were to be sent to Clemente for future consideration. The apartment over the studio would be allocated for his Aunt Louise's living quarters, but ownership would fall to him via a living will.

Clemente asked many questions, but Tony answered none. Tony only asked one question: which bank had his dad used? That bank would be designated for payments owed. He also wanted to know where the royalties were and how much had been earned. Payments for LeCroix's salary would also include Clemente's fees. If, for some reason, he felt anyone was "trying to rip him off," he'd turn all matters over to the state attorney general and the state bar association.

Next, he phoned Bill West and told him what to do with the $75,000.00. He also wanted another $25,000.00 sent to his bank in Cripple Creek and a credit card with no limit included.

He then phoned his Chief of Police and asked if Detective Lee O'Kelly could accompany him on a mission in Little Rock and for an additional week on the Eastern Seaboard. He would serve as an officer aiding in protective measures for his mayor. His expenses and overtime would be paid by Citizen Tony Gianni and not the city. A city vehicle would be used for this mission.

While in Little Rock, they would meet with a group that wanted to bid on golf courses in Cripple Creek and an amusement park developer that wanted to pursue building a special park in Cripple Creek.

After these meetings, Officer O'Kelly would accompany the mayor on trips to New York City, Miami, Florida, and perhaps the country of Belize. They expected to return within two weeks. The Police Chief agreed and assigned O'Kelly to the mayor immediately. The mayor told him to be aware that he wanted him armed.

Tony knew he'd need money, a passport, legal representation, and personal protection. He'd take care of all arrangements. The next thing he needed was a representative to handle entertainment endeavors. That would be Mr. Mark Musial of Nashville, Tennessee, who was known as an entertainment license attorney. Tony's tax attorney in Little Rock would have Musial fly out to Little Rock to meet with Tony and himself regarding matters that centered around city business and Tony's personal business and affairs.

He phoned Samantha just as Lee O'Kelly arrived. "Come on in. I'll explain what must be done in a few minutes. Right now, I'm on the phone with the City Manager," said Tony.

"Samantha, I got word last night my parents are dead, and I must return to New York to take care of a lot of items. Lee O'Kelly is going with me, but first, we'll stop in Little Rock to meet about the golf courses and the entertainment attraction people. We'll take a plane to New York and handle family business. There is a possibility we'll go to Miami and maybe Belize to take care of some of my business. Now, I'll pay Lee for his services after we leave Little Rock. I shall pay all expenses. Along the way, I'll meet with Mark Musial, who is the foremost entertainment attorney in Nashville. I'll pay his fees as well since the majority of his duties will be for me."

"When will you leave?" she asked.

"Tonight. We'll be staying at the Capitol Marriott if they have rooms available. Please have someone call ahead and make reservations for me. Use cell phone #2 while I'm gone. For the public, freeze calls."

"Sure, consider it done," she said.

Then he called Lee into his office and told him what was going on and why he was in peril.

"Hell, boss, don't you think we need another cop with us?"

"Yes, I suspect we do, but are you trying to tell me something?" Tony asked.

"Look, I used to be an NYPD street cop and know another cop in New York who works as a private detective. He and I were in Iran in the Marines together, and with one phone call, I can contact Bud Griffin to lease a limousine and pick us up from the next plane arriving from Little Rock and Mr. Musial from the next plane from Nashville, provided both flights land at LaGuardia.

Okay, boss, you call Mr. Musial and have him look out for a limo representing you, and we'll all take the trip to your dad's studio, take care of business there, then head to Mr. Clemente, provided he'll be in his office, and then back to LaGuardia for either Miami or Belize. We'll need four plane tickets to either place. You'll tell us where.

What do you think of what I just said, especially the part about Bud?" asked Lee.

"Do it, especially the part about Bud. I'll call the Ocean Festival company to learn where we need to go and meet with the CEO of Ocean Festival," said Tony.

Both men made the calls, and it all worked out well. To reach the CEO of Ocean, they would need to see his attorneys in Miami first. If it would be just a signature, they could send Musial on down to Belize, and the rest could be handled from there.

The next day, they packed, went by his bank, and collected twenty thousand dollars in cash, thirty thousand in travel checks, and his long-awaited no-limit credit card. Then they departed for Little Rock.

While Tony was meeting with the golf and amusement park people, Lee went to the airport and made arrangements for LaGuardia. He also phoned Mr. Musial and alerted him to travel to New York, where the limo would pick him up.

In the meantime, Tony decided not to build a municipal golf course at this time but agreed on the amusement park production. He called Samantha and told her what he had done. The Ferris wheel would be first, and she needed to call them and issue a P.O. Work would begin as soon as the area was graded and planned. The company would take care of the rest.

The next item would be the merry-go-round. It was understood that the people who would operate all rides and manage the park would be hired by the city. He asked her to call a city council meeting to begin a new budget order, adopting the parks and recreation department to have control over the functions of the arrangements he had made. She was also to contact the newspaper to announce the news of everything he had explained to her.

Bud was everything Lee had said he was—big, strong, a veteran, and smart. He was not afraid of anything because he knew how to organize. Mr. Musial was not timid and gave advice on the studio.

Tony's dad had been a pop music producer. To make money now, Musial advised him to convert the studio over to country music and hire someone in Nashville to run his business.

"Should I transfer the studio to Nashville, to my place in Cripple Creek, or just leave it in New York?" Tony asked.

"Wherever you can watch over it the best," Musial answered.

"In that case, I'll hire someone in Nashville to move to Arkansas, and together we'll convert over to country and figure out a way to make money at it," said Tony.

Musial gave him the name and number of Sonny Gibson, an A&R expert who could help him. That would be phone call number one. But first, he went into the studio in New York and met with LeCroix, who was belligerent to everyone until Tony told him, "Get your things and get out. You're fired."

Tony just didn't like him and got rid of him at once. To make sure he left, Tony gave him two things: $200.00 and a right cross. When he came to, Bud and Lee tossed him onto the street. Bud made him turn over the keys to the building while Tony went upstairs to see Aunt Louise and told her the studio would be moved to his home.

"Aunt Louise, you may live here for the rest of your life. I'm going to appoint a real estate company to rent the old studio out and take care of the upkeep, as well as your apartment. I've got to leave now, and be advised—I kicked LeCroix out. Never let him back in."

On the way to LaGuardia, Tony informed Musial to go on to Miami and get the situation with the cruise ship in order. "If there is any type of problem, go on to their other headquarters in Belize for final arrangements."

The two men agreed that Ocean Festival owed Tony $275,000 and that in the following months, rental payments should be mailed to Musial for distribution.

Musial then told Tony about a casino for sale in Atlantic City if he wanted to consider buying it.

Chapter 19

Tony had two other people he wanted to see before he returned to Cripple Creek. First, here in New York, his daughter and grandson. Then he and Lee would fly to Birmingham, rent a car, and drive to Tuscaloosa to see Bea and Bobby. He had Bud locate his daughter and grandson, then take a car from "Little Italy," with Bud driving to the "Taj Mahal" Casino in Atlantic City. He went on to LaGuardia and put Musial on a plane to Miami. He caught a small rental plane to Atlantic City and prepared a suite for them as he waited.

That afternoon, they arrived. Much to his chagrin, Annette came along. His daughter's name was Patricia, and his grandson was Anthony. Annette looked much better than the last time he had seen her.

"Hi, Tony. Damn, you look good. Where are you living now?" she asked.

He didn't answer. He was staring at his daughter, who was beautiful, and his grandson, who looked like him.

"Welcome, all. Come on in," he said.

His daughter embraced him, and his grandson extended his hand for a handshake. Annette just stared at him. Again, she asked personal questions.

"Are you married, and why are you here?"

"No, not married, no other children, and the reason I'm here is to shut down my dad's recording studio. I was told someone wants to sell me this casino, and I'll talk to them this evening," said Tony.

"What kind of business are you in now, Tony?" asked Annette.

Bud spoke up. "He's the mayor of a city in the Midwest."

She showed her astonishment with a gaping "O." Patricia and Anthony started laughing. Soon, all were laughing. Tony just beamed. They showed pride in him.

Patricia said, "Tell us about it."

"I won a lot of land in the northwest corner of a state and built homes for folks who wanted to have a second home to enjoy a lot of sporting events. One thing led to another, and now I've built a city of about twelve thousand. The governor appointed me as mayor. Now, y'all tell me what y'all do."

Patricia started laughing again. "Y'all? Are you a southern hick now?"

"Yes, I am, and proud of it," he said. "No joke, what do you do for a living, Patricia?"

"I work in a department store for ladies. Anthony is an office manager for the New York Mets baseball team."

"How about you, Annette?"

"I work for Uncle Turk at his kiosk on Jones Beach. Not much, but I make a living. Never married."

Tony had ordered dinner to be sent up to the suite for the five of them. It included lobster, steak, and all the trimmings. The bar was stocked, but he had very little to drink. Annette had several scotch and sodas, but the rest only had wine and beer.

Tony was impressed to learn that Patricia had graduated from NYU and that Anthony was working on getting into Annapolis. Annette never went to college, but she had always worked for the family. During the conversation, he learned his father had helped with Patricia's college tuition.

The family got to know each other throughout the night but took a break to attend a show featuring Roy Clark in the main room. To everyone's surprise but Tony and Bud's, Roy Clark came up to their suite. The two men excused themselves and went into the bedroom to talk. Within a few minutes, they re-entered, and Clark embraced Tony just before departing.

"Hey, Tony, what was all that about?" Annette asked.

"Well, I'm moving Dad's old studio to Cripple Creek and hired Sonny Gibson to run it. If it is going to make money in the future, it must specialize in country music. I just hired Roy Clark to be my first 'star,' and he's coming out in about three months to get started with us. In addition to his music, I'll get a portion of his concert earnings, sales of T-shirts, hats, etc. He'll help me sign up a stable of singers and musicians. I'd like to sign at least three beautiful female singers. I wish to keep them in Cripple Creek if I could," said Tony.

The next day, he had Bud return them to New York and turn the limo in. He phoned Pete and had him send a truck to New York to unhook and load up the studio, including the outside sign, and bring it to Cripple Creek to be placed downtown near Cowboy Way Street.

He told his only family farewell and caught a flight to Birmingham, but first, he talked to the attorney of Donald Trump, owner of the casino, and made a counteroffer for ownership. Anthony told him he would notify him if he got selected to attend the Naval Academy. Tony was very proud of him. Trump would phone him tonight with an answer. The offer wasn't enough, so no deal.

Again, he rented a car and drove to Tuscaloosa. Bea, Bobby, and Bobby's wife, Alicia, met him at Dreamland for lunch.

Bea spoke first. "Hi, Tony. Long timenosee. Where have you been?"

He explained it all while they ate together and spent the remainder of the day talking about Gail and now his family.

They didn't give out any of their business, but Tony noticed Bea had no rings on her left finger. She mentioned she had a new job at a jeweler's store. She did ask him, however, if he was married.

"No wonder—you've been so busy since we last met. I guess when you were last here, I was engaged. He changed his mind and moved to Texas. I guess I'm just going to be an old maid," she said.

Alicia had majored in accounting at Bama, but jobs just didn't pay much here.

"I'm looking for a new job that would work well for Bobby and me," she said.

Bobby was also looking for a good job. His degree was in Economics. He seemed to be someone who could manage any type of business. However, none had been available that would show him a future.

"Bobby, my city needs a Human Resource Director. I'm offering it to you. Plus, you and Alicia will have a three-bedroom plush house to live in, and you won't have to make house payments for a year.

"Alicia, I have a job for you as my accountant for all the businesses I own. I need you to start the day you arrive so that we may find you an office and hire a secretary.

"Bea, I need a Director of Christian Actions. You will move into a building we're constructing now that can house the YMCA and YWCA. Those two groups will start housing homeless people and families. You will have a two-bedroom bungalow near Bobby and Alicia's home. Your salary will be equal to that of a department head who works for the city.

"I do have a daughter and grandson, but if I offered them jobs, it would be the same as yours."

Bea started weeping profusely for two to three minutes. Bobby tried to quiet her, but no way would she stop until Tony wrapped her in his arms.

"Tony, how can someone be as good as you?"

"I'm not good, I think. I just care for all of you, and God has given me opportunities to help a lot of people, y'all included."

Alicia hesitated. "But, Tony—"

"Do y'all want the job or not?" Tony said with a grin.

All three said yes together.

"Settle up here and hire movers to load you up and come to Cripple Creek, Arkansas, on Highway 412. Here's some traveling money."

He gave them $5,000.

Chapter 20

Tony drove to Cripple Creek from Tuscaloosa through Memphis and then on home. He got there that night and crashed. The next morning, he called Samantha and Mark Musial's office in Nashville.

Samantha called him back with a lot of problems that needed his attention. Plus, she wanted to know what he'd decided about the golf courses and amusement park.

"Samantha, what do you think about placing the municipal golf course near the apartment complex area, south of the residential/church area, very near the Boston Mountains National Park? A piece of that would be near the river also. Think of the amusement park and Ferris wheel at Casey's old building. Shell Oil wants to be on the strip, and I agree about that location. Tell Casey the city will buy his area, destroy it, and make the amusement park larger. Did the council vote in the Parks and Recreation Department?" Tony asked.

"Yes, but we'll need a director. Do you have anyone in mind?" she asked.

"Not really. We need someone who will be an asset, just as we did when we got the other chiefs. We need a Citizen Senior Center at the YMCA area. Place that center as part of the Parks and Recreation Department. The amusement park, Ferris wheel, arcade, and merry-go-round should all be under Parks and Recreation. We need to build a baseball, soccer, and youth football complex on my land near the forthcoming country club. I wish for each Tuesday morning at the country club, the seniors have an opportunity to play there. We need a lot of directors and managers to be hired in order to help our citizens. I possibly have a Parks and Recreation Director. He'll be here tomorrow with his wife and mother.

They are good friends of mine. As a matter of fact, they'll live at my home until they make some decisions," replied Tony.

"Do I know them?" she asked.

"No, but do you remember me talking about my friend I was in the Army with, the one that got killed?"

"Yeah, Hershel was his name, wasn't it?" she asked.

"Yes, it's his wife and their son, plus the son's wife, Alicia."

"What's the boy's name?" she asked.

"Well, he really isn't a boy. He's about 23 or 24, named Bobby, and graduated with honors from the University of Alabama. He majored in economics and minored in business administration. In a roundabout way, I've offered him the job, but he's never been tested in the business world. He works at a bank now but isn't wild about it. I want you to ask pertinent questions when we all get together. His wife is a pearl. Remember, she is an accountant. Bobby could make a good Human Resources Director. Check him out on that too."

He phoned Mr. Musial back and found out some quick information. The check was for $375,000.00, and he would send it immediately, less his fee of fifteen percent.

"Mr. Musial, I need to keep you on a lengthy retainer. I'm moving my New York studio here to Cripple Creek, and I feel like I must have an experienced entertainment attorney to work for me. I've hired Sonny Gibson to run this operation, and I need you and him to fly out here next Wednesday. Since you're coming anyway, I need you to check around Nashville and find me a small passenger jet, not only for my use but for the hospital, city, and passenger use. It needs to seat twenty passengers. Certainly, we'll need at least two pilots to start with. As soon as you find one, let me know."

"You ask a lot. I'll let you know about my decisions when I come out on Wednesday," Musial said.

He called Sonny Gibson and asked him to ride out with Mr. Musial and gave him Musial's phone number. He did all of this without knowing if the airstrip had been made. He then called Pete Oats and learned it was completed except for striping, and he'd have it done by Tuesday at noon.

That Friday, Tony took Stella and Roman on a short trip to the site of the country club, residential area, and sportsplex for youth sports. He was the owner of the property and felt all of these constructions would be essential for the area. The music impact would bring in a lot of new citizens. Roman did some sketches and would contact their architect for future considerations.

Roman asked the first and probably the most important question, "How many more people will this bring into our city?"

"Well, the music part will not bring in as many as you'd think. We have to designate it in two sizes: permanent party and temporary party. People who will make records, travel with stars, and do local concerts should be about eight families. These folks will want to be a part of the country club. Maybe five families of stars will live here. We probably need to build a half dozen condos for many of them. With their involvement, I guess we'll need to add another police and fire station. I have family moving here that would prefer living in this area. We'll need roads, streets, sidewalks, and maybe another park, which would be near the sportsplex," said Tony.

"Wait just a damn minute, Mr. Mayor. Did you say family? I didn't know you had one," asked Samantha.

"Yeah, she's right," said Roman.

He just smiled and said, "My daughter, Patricia, and her son, Anthony. Anthony may be leaving here, though, to enter the Naval Academy. His grandmother, Annette, possibly will move here. I also am having my friend Hershel's widow, Bea, and her son, Bobby, move here. We could use Bobby—smart man—who could move into some position working for the city.

I know I can find jobs for the women. One has a degree in accounting, the other runs the Christian Action Group," he said.

On the way back to City Hall, Mark Musial called Tony to give him much-needed information. "Found you a Cessna nineteen-passenger jet with someone excited to be living in Cripple Creek rather than Nashville. He'll bring me in the jet that we've been talking about. Now, I still haven't made a decision about working full-time for you. Just give me more time," said Musial.

"Understand, but could you arrange for Roy Clark to visit here soon?" asked Tony.

"Glad to. I think he's in Canada on tour now. I'll talk to him once he gets back," he said.

That afternoon, Bea, Bobby, and Alicia arrived in town. Tony took them to his home, and they were so impressed.

"Tony, this is the most beautiful home I've ever seen. Jefferson would have been happy with what you've done. I was afraid on the way up that we'd have to sleep on a cot," she said, laughing.

After a meal, Tony took them on a tour of the city. Again, they were impressed and ooh-ed and ahh-ed over everything they could see and what was to be built.

That night over dinner, Tony told Bobby about the two jobs that were coming available: Parks and Recreation Director or Human Resources Director. The pay would be virtually the same, but the hours for Parks and Recreation would be longer. Tony explained that he thought Bobby qualified for either.

"If I have a choice, I believe being the Human Resources Director would align with my education and the job I now hold," said Bobby.

His wife and mother nodded in agreement, and so did Tony.

"Alicia, we have a job available working as an accountant in our Accounting Department. Normally, in the city scheme of things, there isn't as much cash flow as in personal business. However, we added the utilities cash flow to our banking collections. Our accountant, Ken, needs help appropriating purchase orders but wishes to transfer those duties to Human Resources when a director is hired."

"Do your departments need to ask for a P.O. each time they buy something?" she asked.

"Only when the amount exceeds $1,000.00. Then the director asks the council for permission in accordance with the budget. I'm the worst violator of our budgets, but Ken has really helped me adjust. I underwrite with my own money for any department without following procedures—I need to stop that," he said with a smile.

Bea interrupted, "In front of City Hall is a statue of you as the founder of this city. You've only been here three years, and what you have done is unbelievable. Therefore, I'm sure the statue is well earned."

"Three other people, who then multiplied into six, then thirty-six, helped me get this city on the move. I just owned the land, and we started there."

Bobby asked, "What do you mean you owned the land?"

"I won thousands of acres of property on the bank of White River, plus a cabin I lived in until I built this glorious house. I then started building in many ways. The city still owes me millions of dollars for properties I've allowed them to build on—you know, like City Hall, the Police Department, etc.," he said.

"Wow," said Bea.

"Listen, y'all, for some unknown reason, God is using me to do the right things. I started out just needing a place to stay, and before I knew it, three other people and I began this city. Now they are my dearest friends—friends I can and do trust.

"The only woman I've ever loved was killed by someone who thought I was driving the car she was in. I had given her the car, and one night, she was shot to death. I won this land here in a poker game, and I won a lot of money in a poker game while at sea. The ship I was gambling on was included in the profits from the proceeds. I now own a cruise ship and get paid rental each time it is used. Maybe all of you can take a cruise on it sometime.

"Let me explain this now—I don't gamble anymore because it would involve innocent people, and I never want to harm anyone," said Tony.

Bea, teary-eyed, looked at Tony with warmth and compassion. "You are one in a million, Tony Gianni. When my husband met you, it was evident then that you are a true friend."

Bobby, jokingly, said, "Don't want the job—want to marry you!"

All the people screamed with laughter. Tony actually turned red with embarrassment.

Chapter 21

Tony got the Tuscaloosa family squared away with their jobs and housing. However, he was so busy with other activities that he didn't spend much time with them. They adapted quickly to the community and moved their "letter" to the First Methodist Church. As a matter of fact, all the churches built fine-looking sanctuaries. The Catholic cathedral would take longer because it was being built of marble and other stones. Special stonemasons were brought in to do the work. The Christian Action "Factory," which included the YMCA and YWCA, was about a third of the way toward completion. It was ideal for Bea.

Patricia phoned her dad just to check up on him. At that time, he was finishing up the airport and had fallen in love with his jet. Three other members of the community were pilots and owned small single-engine propeller aircraft, and he was told the new doctor moving in owned a "Sky Courier" twin-engine.

As this was being completed, at a council meeting, the discussion for a hospital was brought up. Families living here went to Fayetteville for hospital care, but it was a real inconvenience, and some specialty services were wanted, such as a cancer center, VA clinic, maternity ward, and adequate emergency rooms. Four big businesses, including city employees, had proper insurance for hospital care. It would probably pay for itself as well as attract physicians.

He asked her about his grandson and whether he was accepted to Annapolis. He could hear her laughter when she told him yes. His next question was, "Would you be interested in moving to Cripple Creek and being the manager and part-owner of a 'famous' recording studio?"

"Tony, let me visit first. You know I've never lived in a small town, plus being with you... After all, you've never been a part of my life, and I don't know how to handle that. What about Mom? And where will Anthony visit when he has leave?"

Tony reacted at once. "I now have a personal jet plane that I can send to gather you for a week of looking everything over and to meet the people."

"I suppose I could do that, but where will I stay?" she asked.

"In my house. We can have some time to get acquainted, plus meet my close friends," he said.

"What about your wife or girlfriend? What will she say about my visiting?" she asked.

"No wife, never had one, and no girlfriend. She was killed," he said.

"Okay, how about next week?" she asked.

"I'll give your number to my pilots, and they'll pick you up, probably in New Jersey. I understand that's the ideal place to collect passengers for small aircraft," he said.

"What clothing should I bring?" she asked.

"Casual—jeans, pantsuits, no coats, just a sweater. Hell, honey, you don't need clothes. I'll buy you what you need. By the way, we're opening a new dance hall, and you're my date. As mayor, I must be at each grand opening. I know I'll need to buy you clothing there. It's a country-western facility," he said.

"Looking forward to the visit. Always wondered about you," she said.

"You'll find out I'm more Southern in talk, actions, and beliefs. But Patricia, you'll receive a lot of strange questions from the citizens and my friends. In the meantime, I suggest you buy

Billboard Magazine, *Music Magazine*, and any magazines or newspapers that have anything to do with country music. Check around and find out if any country stars are appearing in New York. Let me know, and I'll have my secretary get you a couple of tickets for the event. She'll handle all features and seating," he said.

"Wow, you must be important," she said.

"Not really, but I know the right people in the right situations. Goodbye, dear. Write this number down—it's my secretary's phone, and she'll handle the details."

He phoned his secretary, who was now Sandra Allen, and told her what to do. She handled all the details, plus phoning the Western Clothing Store and instructing them to order clothing for Patricia since she had gotten her sizes, including her boot size.

He went into City Hall to meet with a long list of people who needed to speak to their mayor, and he needed to talk to the city council and the city's physicians about building a hospital. At one time, a group of people wanted to have the city build a minor league baseball stadium, but necessity dictated building a hospital instead. The city had a small clinic, but Cripple Creek now had a population of over twelve thousand, plus visitors coming in for various events, which would increase the total to about twenty thousand.

He got a note from his real estate company that there were only a few existing homes available. The new subdivision near the proposed country club had started, with massive soil grading for all forthcoming construction. The condos and apartments on the northeast side of town were being built. The chalets on the mountain were in place, but they were expensive, and the road to connect them with not only the plateau but also each other wasn't being built at this time. An engineer who had experience building on mountains was needed. He would get Roman to handle that project.

The city needed two other construction companies that could be housed at the industrial park. The city also needed schools to be finished as soon as possible. The engineers Tony had hired to build the sports complex and the golf courses should arrive at any time. "Cowboy Way" was nearing completion. Tater Graham, Western Clothing, Arkansas Saddle and Tack, Rosita's, and Memphis Bar-B-Que were completed.

Next year, a concert hall would be built near the end of Market Road. Kiosks should be built by the end of November. This year, for the first time, a gigantic pine Christmas tree would be erected on top of the mountain. Tony decided to allow the citizens of Cripple Creek to name the mountain later. It should be an omnificent sight once all factors were built or mounted.

It was somewhat like the Arch in St. Louis, the Statue of Liberty, and the sculpture of Sitting Bull in configuration. The mountain should have more of a façade than either a zip line or ski slope could provide. Again, he'd let the people of Cripple Creek have a voice in choosing. Yet, as he owned the mountain and not the city, he appreciated their input.

The *Cripple Creek Register*, the city's only newspaper, was a strong proponent of a "classy" identification for the mountain and would conduct the poll without involving the mayor. They were aware of the ownership. The publisher, Guy Archer, was an Arkansas graduate and had worked at one time with the *St. Louis Dispatch*. The newspaper wasn't, at this time, tied to any big-time network or other identifying news outlets.

The interview was a bust. Just do the poll.

Tony's Sky Courier, a twin-engine, nineteen-seat aircraft, descended at the airport in good time. Sandra Allen picked Patricia up and did the customary tour on the way to her dad's home. Along the way, Sandra told Patricia a lot of information about her dad.

"He came up here from Biloxi and lived a few weeks on the banks of the river in an old fishing cabin. He met a few guys plus a banker in Fayetteville who encouraged him to enter the real estate business. He built and sold beautiful houses that added charm to this little village. The local friends talked him into building this city because your dad had leadership, bravery, and money. The banker especially liked him and was a crony of Governor Huckabee, pushing a lot of deals through. Tony had old friends who popped in and advised him on what to do. Architects were his best friends, and he paid them to get the ball rolling. So within a year, a city was formed, and the governor swore your dad in as mayor. I work for him as his secretary and am really like his right-hand man. Our police department reveres him completely. The jet you were on will be picking up another employee for the police department and singer Roy Clark when and if we return you to New York. This guy will be the assistant chief of police," said Sandra.

"What about his social life or hobbies?" asked Patricia.

"As far as I know, there isn't any. The man owns a cruise ship but has never been on it," said Sandra.

"A cruise ship?" Patricia asked, astonished.

"Yes, and see that mountain over there?" She pointed out the car window to the right side.

"Yeah, what about it?" asked Patricia.

"He owns that too!" said Sandra.

"All of that money, and he still isn't married?" said Patricia. "Why not? What happened to his true love? He had one once, didn't he?"

"Yes, he only loved one woman, a lady in Biloxi, who was shot to death," said Sandra.

They arrived at Tony's house, and Patricia screeched at the glory.

"Tony, how and why did you build such a magnificent house on this sparkling river?" asked Patricia as she exited Sandra's car and saw her dad standing on the back porch. Toby came running up and bounded into Tony's arms as he was trying to embrace Patricia.

"Tony, may I start calling you Daddy?" Patricia asked.

"Honey, of course. That is if it is okay with Toby," said Tony.

Sandra said, "Boss, I like Patricia."

"Me too," said Tony. "Let's all go in. Let me help with the luggage. Sandra, I have reservations for the three of us at the Grist Mill. Could you get your boyfriend to join us?"

"I'll try, but I don't know if he is working late today. They have a rush order of eight trucks to be delivered to Raleigh, North Carolina, that needs to be completed as soon as possible. It's for the city departments, and all are blood red," Sandra said.

Tony brought Patricia in and placed her luggage in the guest suite. Sandra phoned her boyfriend, Jimmy, a mechanic who installs shock absorbers on each truck at the Ayastigi plant.

The three met in the bar of the mansion and had mixed drinks. In between being so excited about the trip and her dad's house, Patricia told all about Anthony at the Naval Academy. She told her dad she thought that when he graduated from school, he'd try to become a Navy pilot by going through training in Pensacola. He told his daughter how proud he was of him.

They went to the Grist Mill for steaks, and joining them was Roman Pascal. It only took two drinks apiece before it became evident that it was love at first sight between Patricia and Roman. Sandra sat there, bewildered at how this became a reality.

That evening at home, Patricia asked all about the record studio. She told Tony how she had been doing her research on country music. She wanted to know all about Sonny Gibson and if he was going to rebuild the studio here. She also told her dad she had attended a concert at Madison Square Garden that featured Johnny Paycheck and a Mexican singer named Freddie Fender, who was very good. She bought their CDs but hadn't played them yet. Another guy performed that night, a big man from Alabama named Sonny James. "I liked them all. I think you've got the right idea. We need to be a part of all concerts and sales. Big money there. I know you said you'd get me free tickets, but I wanted to experience the concert scene. There is something we both must experience, and that is to take a trip to Nashville on a Saturday night and attend the Grand Ole Opry."

"I want you and me to sit down with this Sonny Gibson guy and find out how to make this record business successful. What's the deal with this guy, Roy Clark? Have you signed him yet?" she asked.

"No, but I'm sure he'll be our 'bell cow.' He is very talented—probably the most talented. I would like for him to bring his band here to open at 'Tater Grahams,'" said Tony.

"May I go and visit 'Famous' studio tomorrow?" Patricia asked.

"Yes, but I'll get Roman to take you. He's building everything—places to mount keyboards and other echo chambers. Believe me, Patricia, a lot goes into recording music. We'll start with CDs, tapes, and six tracks. Best sound is what we'll put our money on."

The next day at lunch, Roman came by, picked her up, and they ate lunch at a catfish restaurant. Afterward, they went to the studio. Roman showed her around and, should she take the job, where her office would be. It was there they had their first kiss. She melted like an Eskimo pie on a hot Mississippi day. He was woozy too. He took her to City Hall to see her daddy and meet his workers there.

She walked into his office, closed the door, and locked it. He leaned back in his executive chair, looked up into her lovely eyes, and asked, "What's on your mind, honey?"

"Do you realize what you've done in my life recently?" she asked.

"I think so, but you tell me!"

"First of all, I have found my father, and you know what? I not only like him, but I love him. The job you've offered seems to be great, and I accept. I will live here. Third, I've fallen in love with another man, Roman! He is perfect, and he's in love with me. Fourth, my son called today and told me he is happy too. Fifth, my mother does not want to follow me here. Hooray! She has been a pain in my ass forever. I've always wanted my dad, and now I've got him, and she isn't around telling me to hate him. No fucking way. My dad is stuck with me for the remainder of his life," she said.

"Young lady, if you use profanity again, I'll wash your mouth out," he said.

"Yeah, and I bet you would," she said, smiling.

He stood, and they grabbed each other in a tremendous bear hug, both shedding a "lake" of tears.

The next day, he took her to look at one of the new houses almost finished in the subdivision near the country club. It was an English manor-type with a large garage. She accepted it, and Tony financed it. She would move in shortly after returning with her furniture left in New York. She would drive over from her New York home to her new home, new job, and her dad, which would present her with a new, changed life—hopefully with her new husband… Roman!

She, like her father, had made it through a strange battlefield. A month later, Roman proposed to her.

Chapter 22

General Ambrose and the Corps of Engineers took great pride in dredging and removing so many obstacles from the White River that included all of Madison County. The residents of Cripple Creek and Huntsville, Arkansas, took him in as one of their own and introduced him to a way of life he had never known.

He had grown up in St. Louis in a large family that balanced on poverty and social acceptance seemingly forever. He worked part-time as a landscaper for the estate owned by the beer baron, August Busch. In addition to working like an adult, he had to walk from his home in Soldier's Heights to the riches of the Busch family. Many times, he hid behind some bushes on the way and took a nap. His breakfast before school consisted of garbage "leftover food." Since he "rubbed elbows" with the gentry, he was welcomed to walk through their properties. Many mothers of his friends, whom he had met along these paths, realized his plight and left many articles of clothing for him to better himself with. He bathed during the summer in a small creek that ran parallel to his paths. During the winter, he sneaked into the Busch brewery and bathed in the cleanup baths there.

He was always alone, but in his paths to decency, he hid many objects he had found at various points, like toothbrushes, combs, talcum powder, and many pennies that subsidized him. He arrived at most of his destinations on time and looking as though he had lived among the upper middleclass.

At an abandoned cottage on his trek was his home away from home. There was no furniture there except for an old iron stove left behind. He could hide there, stoke the stove, and keep warm during snowy or rainy days. He used to imagine this was his home and used this address when he registered for school. Yes, he did go home daily wearing the clothing he had departed from home wearing that morning. His family knew he worked when not attending classes. His frivolity with his classmates gave him acceptance, especially because he was so adept at games and sports.

There was only one problem, though. He had fallen in love at the age of twelve with Megan Bush-Carter, granddaughter of the leader of the infamous clan of brewers. She left him notes everywhere. Once, when he was taking on a side job as a paperboy for the St. Louis Post-Dispatch, she came up to his street corner, took his hand, led him to an entranceway where no one could see them, and kissed him like adults do. He fell completely in love with this wonderful and beautiful German-American. She would, at any opportunity, run up to him and kiss him quickly.

But her mystique reached high proportions when she arrived for high school. Her parents were planning on sending her off to an all-girls school in Chicago. She agreed to go there without a problem, provided her dad helped the Ambrose kid get into West Point. She had learned he was a straight-A student and that his family could not afford to send him to college. Her father agreed he would help if the boy's own family filled out the paperwork in advance. She went to her principal's office and had him get her what she needed. It was then she realized a senator or congressman must endorse the candidate for acceptance. Now she was really in a pickle. Her father hated politics.

It was now time to be honest about the situation, so she invited Ambrose McCall to come into her home, meet her father in his study, and tell him, "You want to go to West Point for an education, and when you graduate, you wish to marry me." He blanched at this notion, but he did it, and the old man went all the way in his endeavors, including giving her away to Ambrose at the largest wedding anyone had ever witnessed in St. Louis.

While he was away in Korea, working as an engineer in the Army, angels came and took her and her child away. He then lost all his family except the U.S. Army. Now, he was living alone in the garden apartment of the home he and Megan once owned.

After he returned from Korea, the family never treated him badly but just did not have time for him. He remained in the Army until the proper retirement age. However, his job as an engineer serving his nation did not stop. He was still needed and was retained in an Army/Civilian job, working project to project. This is how he met Tony Gianni and began the rest of his life with the friend he wished was his son.

"General, Tony Gianni. How are you, sir?" said Tony.

"Fine, Mr. Mayor, and you?" was his answer.

"Fine, but I've been concerned. I haven't heard from you lately. I called your office, and they say it appears you are going to stick with this second retirement you've imposed. What are you doing now?" Tony asked.

There was a semi-long pause before the retiree, in a muffled voice, said, "Think it's time to call it a day. Couldn't seem to please the young men in Washington, so I figure I'd just stay in my condo in St. Louis."

"What you're going to do there is what, wilt… Forget the age thing, General. You're needed. If you wonder where—well, by God, right here in Cripple Creek," said Tony.

"It's this way. We need another city councilman, and those that need you have recommended you move down, live here another year doing something, and next year run for office as one of our city councilmen. By living here a year, you will become a citizen of Cripple Creek. For the first year you're here, you'll work from my real estate office, and your project will be to construct a concert theatre somewhere near the base of the mountain. You may call me back at this number if you wish today. I'll be at my desk."

"I'll answer that now. And it is a resounding 'yes.' Expect me on the first of the month. Got a question, though—where will I stay?"

"For the beginning, here with me at my house. Later, at a condo at the country club. By the way, one of your other 'perks' will be a four-wheel drive vehicle and membership at the country club."

Laughing, the General said, "You really know how to please a girl."

He called Bea and told her how her deceased husband's commanding general was moving to her city and that upon the General's arrival, he would host a dinner party for about thirty people at the mansion. She was ecstatic at all he had told her.

"Tony," she asked, "will it be formal?"

"Guess you might call it semi-formal. I'll have Sandra or someone send out invitations. Naturally, we'll invite Bobby and Alicia. Your dinner date will be the General."

Sandra began that evening composing the guest list for the dinner party. The mayor had listed some old friends he had met when he first arrived in Arkansas. Among them were Nigel, George, Bill, his pilots, the existing city council, Jeff Powers, Pete Oats, Roman and Patricia, department chiefs, all of the "Famous" recording staff, managers of the big industrial plants, and his date for the evening, Miss Susan Bay Smith, his second signee as a recording artist for "Famous" Recording.

The next night at Tater Graham's, she and Roy Clark would open the show for a concert, and then the group "Cripple Creek" would be the house band. The quest now would be for another candidate for the Fourth District Councilman or Councilwoman. Perhaps they would be at the party, she thought.

Sandra, of course, was invited, but she was unsure if her date would attend. They were in love with each other, but her job, firmly white-collar, was vastly different from his, which was blue-collar.

However, he and the mayor were great friends. Even though he worked on an assembly line, he held the power of a shift foreman. He had a degree from Arkansas State in business and had played football there. His name was Jimmy Bowling, and he would be an asset for any vocation or office. Tony felt so, at least, even though Jimmy did not.

Nevertheless, Tony phoned him and almost demanded that he appear at the function. Reluctantly, he agreed. You just didn't say no to Tony Gianni.

Now that he was attending, Tony went to work on arranging a group to ask Jimmy to run for office as the fifth councilman. He selected Casey, Jimmy's boss; Pick Oscar Pounders; Elizabeth; and Todd. He needed Jimmy to be the council member over the industrial and eastern section of the city. He had moved here from Jonesboro, Arkansas, and met Sandra at church. Pick Oscar was totally in agreement. The city had been good to his plant, and the Japanese owners appreciated when an employee was adaptable to political functions that coincided. Jimmy could handle both. Now the big job would be convincing him to run for office. That question would be answered at the party.

The guest list consisted of old friends, new friends, and family. It was probably the best party ever held in Arkansas. Just as the party was beginning, Governor Huckabee and his daughter Sarah, a beautiful child, landed at the new airport and were fetched by Sandra, who happily brought them to the mansion. The governor shook hands with a few of the guests and spent some time with Tony, General Ambrose, and Jimmy before he returned to the airport for a flight to Fort Smith. This was the first time many had ever seen the governor.

Those attending the party were: Casey Powers with Tonya Springs; Elizabeth Black with her husband, Samuel; General Ambrose McCall with Bea McCoy; Patricia Gianni with Roman

Pascal; Bobby McCoy with his wife, Alecia; Samantha with Arnie Patterson; Sandra Allen with Jimmy Bowling; Pete Oats with his wife, Carol; Bill West with his wife, Adele; Lee O'Kelly with his wife, Doris; Bud Griffin with his wife, Victoria. Pick Oscar was in the hospital and had been invited but couldn't attend. Also in attendance were George Barclay with no date; the new fire chief, Jack Reed, with his wife, Lisa; Sonny Gibson with no date; Stella Sands with her date, Ben Trousdale; Ken Antonelli with his wife, Angela; the new Parks and Recreation Director, Karl Kaiser, with his wife, Fay; Utilities Director Cooper Dill with his wife, Charlotte; Adams Tire Co. President Mike Adams with his wife, Jennifer; Arkansas Boat Company Manager Rick Milton with his wife, Ruth; City Attorney Damon Westerly with his wife, Wanda; City Architect Thomas Elliott with his wife, Ann; Cripple Creek Insurance's Paul Rogers with his wife, Wanda; Nigel Gates with his wife, Amber; Cripple Creek Trucking President Victor Sans with his wife, Beth; Arkansas Insurance President Troy Meredith with his wife, Mary; and Senator Jeff Powers with his wife, Susie.

The party was full of fun and a lot of handshaking. The Cripple Creek band played all types of music, and the entire party took place outdoors in the garden and on the back porch. The mayor, with his date Susan Bay Smith, the country singer who had recently signed a contract with "Famous" Studios, conducted the activities.

First was the naming of the proposed country club. The most votes went to the nominated name "Ozark Caverns." The proposed concert auditorium was nominated as the "Southwestern," and the building itself was named "Cripple Creek Hall." All newly appointed chiefs were introduced. The city's most famous tune was the bluegrass song "Cripple Creek," and special introductions were given for the proposed extra city council members, General Ambrose McCall and James Bowling. The crowd cheered at all the announcements, including the legal declaration that, beginning next year, the selection of mayor and council members would be determined by a public vote.

Tony had hired "Dreamland" in Tuscaloosa, Alabama, to cater the meal with ribs and pulled pork. He had flown them up for the cooking and the occasion.

The Cripple Creek Ferris wheel was ready for introduction, and it began with tears in the eyes of Mayor Tony Gianni. "Ladies and gentlemen, I wish to make this known now and forever: the Ferris wheel in Cripple Creek, Arkansas, will be known as 'Casey's Wheel' in honor of the first man who ever asked me to stay here." After that announcement, he phoned the operator, and the wheel was lit and began turning while someone played the city's first song, "Cripple Creek."

Next, he announced, "The trolley fleet will now take all guests to enjoy their first turn on Casey's Wheel! After your ride on Casey's Wheel, don't leave. Instead, get back on your trolley, for you are to be taken to Tater Graham's for a concert and dancing. Beer is on the house. Have some more fun!"

Sonny Gibson topped off the night when he got on stage, took the mic, and said, "Tony Gianni for reelection? Hell, this great man should be our President of the United States!"

Chapter 23

As a proud citizen as well as a proud daughter, she showed her around and answered a "million" questions about her dad, how he came to be here, and about Gail and not Annette. She had been impressed, but not as much as Posto do Sogno and the owner.

At lunch, they arrived a little late; she wanted to get out of the uniform and into something more pleasant. He stood as they approached their table and again looked into her emerald eyes. He just couldn't get over them, but this time, his eyes moved to her luscious lips. "Oh, how I would love to kiss them," he thought. They enjoyed hearty portions of lasagna and salad, but this time, no one drank wine or anything else. Just water.

During the discussion at the table, he overheard Harriet mention she would not be attending the show at the concert due to "she needed to clean up the seating area and bathroom." She laughed and said it was true, "Musicians are the most horrid travelers."

A frown came over Tony's face until Patricia asked him, "What's wrong?"

"You know, it's a tradition. I must introduce all acts on their first time to Cripple Creek's stage," he explained.

"Well, Dad, that's okay. You can ride back out to the plane when Jo Jo drives the bus to load them."

He stuttered and said, "Yeah. I guess I can do that."

Harriet looked disappointed too. Patricia picked up on this, and to have a joke on them, said, "I tell you what, Dad, you do your obligatory introduction, then drive out as soon as possible to the airport and let me have your vehicle while I go back and sign them out, and you help Harriet cleanup."

"Hey, Patricia, who is this Harriet?"

"She's the singer's pilot."

"Hey, girl. That's a good idea! Okay with you, Harriet?"

"Of course," she said, sensing what was happening.

"Hey, Harriet, Patricia and other people have told me attending the Grand 'Ol Opry would be a good thing for me to do and try to meet the 'STARS' for them to realize who I am and about 'famous' studios in Cripple Creek and really what we do that could help them and their families. So, could you go with me?"

"Got you one better. Come on over and ride back with me as I take Marty Robbins after his show to his next gig, which is in Wichita, Kansas."

"Wow, what a great idea. I'll stay the remainder of the night at Roger Miller's hotel when I get back and try to have breakfast with the New Minstrels' lead singer, Kenny Rogers. This way, I have some contact with Marty Robbins, possibly Roger Miller, and Kenny Rogers," he said.

"I'll have you some business cards printed today with your name and position with the studio. Pass them out," Patricia said.

That afternoon, he tried to get building designs for the country club proposed to him. He'd already gotten Stewart Cink's design of the course. He needed to hire a golf pro as well as a club manager.

However, it was hard to concentrate on these duties after he had just met Harriet Hudson. Her face appeared in front of him all day—her light brown hair, perfect face, emerald eyes, gorgeous and sexy body, and her great personality. This was all he knew about her, except she could fly big jet planes. He went home, had a bite to eat, and cleaned up for the concert. At the prescribed time, he went on stage and introduced these guys as if he had known them all his life. He had studied their biographies, learned a little about them, and was informed enough to do a presentable job. He went backstage and watched them for a while, then exited the building, jumped in his car, and dashed off to the airport. He drove up to the ramp of the plane and went in, removing his coat and tie to help her as promised.

She was in the men's lavatory cleaning when he yelled her name. She and Patricia stepped out of a clean place for the musicians to use. Patricia got the keys to the vehicle he was driving and handed him a handful of business cards she had promised.

She departed the ramp, and for the moment, the two who were falling in love just looked at each other. He took two steps forward, and she took three, and before realization set in, they were in each other's arms and kissing. It was a motion each wanted since the first time they felt the aura of the other.

"Tony, it has been many years since I've felt the way I do now," said Harriet. All he could do was moan and place her neck to his lips.

After a few minutes, she said, "As much as I like and understand this, my job as a pilot is to get the engines ready, so excuse me or come up and sit in the co-pilot seat."

He said, "I'll sit in the co-pilot seat unless Randy wishes to talk to me."

"Suit yourself, but once I start flying, I give that my undivided attention," said Harriet.

They just looked at each other and held hands until the rumble of the ramp broke them up. The band was approaching, so Tony got up and got alert. Once they landed in Nashville, ALABAMA got off, and Marty Robbins and his band got on. He arose and went to the co-pilot seat. They flew for about an hour and taxied to the gas area to top off the fuel. Tony stood up to stretch his legs, and she had stepped out to speak to two men on the tarmac. After he used the lavatory, she was back on, as well as Marty and ALABAMA's agents, so they could talk. Tony sat back down and waited.

In the meantime, he overheard the discussion from the agents.

"Sid, what can we do to get some type of guarantee for more income from these souvenir people?"

"Zack, I don't know yet what to do, but I've heard of a group that Roy Clark is with that does a percentage and does all the work. I'll contact Roy about this. I understand he is playing in Charleston, West Virginia."

Hmmm, Tony thought. I'll be calm about this and tell Patricia what I've learned. This way, I won't be putting her in any harmful way, and we can perhaps make money on a special deal.

A real co-pilot got on, and Tony moved to the third seat in the cockpit. Now he was exposed and thought to make the best of a bad situation, so he introduced himself and gave Zack and Sid his business card.

All of a sudden, they became very animated and asked him to go to an area on the plane where they thought they couldn't be heard. Once there, he explained the ten ways he felt they would be happy changing to "Famous." These included:

1. Each artist has an old-fashioned swing band on the road and in the studio. This promises the "Famous" studio sound as well as the artist's sound. Each band has a bandleader who is the only person the artist needs to converse with.

2. On tour: Flight service and other transportation expenses are split 50-50, billed monthly.

3. Handle all souvenir sales and CDs at shows on an 80% artist and 20% "Famous" split. We hire workers and cashiers for this.

4. TV appearances: We receive 20%.

5. Movie appearances: 0% for us.

6. Recording: Something we'd negotiate.

7. Book sales: 0% for us.
8. The door is always open for artists to talk with the studio head and recording head.
9. Your families and you will have medical health benefits.
10. Families and band members will have a place to live with proper medical facilities and excellent education for their children.

Meeting Tony made an impression on each souvenir agent. They met with their employer and shared their experience. Both artists contacted "Famous" about the possibility of signing up with them.

After unloading in Wichita, she dropped Tony off in Nashville, where he had the opportunity to meet Rogers but not Miller before taking a nap. Phoning Patricia and advising her on what he'd learned pleased her and put her on guard for imminent phone calls. He caught his plane and returned home. The city was active, and he was needed again. His staff knew all about Harriet, and those who truly cared for him did not engage in gossip.

He slept soundly that Monday night, and the next morning Patricia phoned him:

"Dad, are you awake?"

"Yes, dear, but I haven't had my coffee yet. Anything wrong?" he replied.

"Quite the contrary! You've apparently awakened Music City. These singers on tour have heard about us and wish to speak with you. Are you up for taking a few calls today at your house, or must you go in for city business?"

"You screen them and give me their numbers, and I'll call from here. However, I must go in just after lunch. Call me at the office this afternoon, and we'll start a plan," he said.

"Heard from Harriet?" she asked.

"No, I'll call her tonight," he said.

"What do you think of her?" she asked.

"Good things. We'll talk about it tonight, okay?"

Sensing his call to duty, she hung up.

Phone calls were made to five different artists, inviting them to visit and bring either their agent or attorney. He explained it would be confidential, and a prototype band and sound would be available. As soon as this was done, he went to his office and had lunch with Samantha to get up to speed on what he should be prepared for.

The hospital situation was coming into focus. Mayo couldn't invest at this time, but a group of orthopedic physicians wanted to arrive that Saturday for more information. He assured Samantha he would be available. He asked her to poll the city council and request their presence if possible. Walmart phoned and inquired about properties to erect a store. She assured them Tony had set aside two locations they could evaluate and decide upon.

Samantha told him that General McCall had stepped in with the contractors of the clubhouse at the country club and had pleased them. Tony had asked the General to do this. The cost factor was adjusted, giving him the leeway to invite membership. As soon as the initiation amount was dictated by links and clubhouse costs, the council and he would begin suggesting membership.

All of this was standard operating procedure. What wasn't standard was the way he felt about Harriet.

That evening, he phoned her three times, but there was no answer. Disappointed? Yes, but understanding her job requirements eased some of his low feelings.

Tuesday morning, as he dressed for work, he heard noise in the kitchen. It was her! She was sitting at the kitchen table, drinking his coffee.

"Hey, you make a good cup of coffee!"

"Oh, baby, it is so good seeing you," he said as he walked across the floor, picked her up, and kissed her deeply.

"I love you, Tony Gianni!" she muttered.

"And I love you, Harriet. I couldn't get an answer last night, and I was afraid you had changed your mind about me," he said.

"No, dear, but we need some time together. My work is becoming a problem, and I need to talk to you about this," she said.

"OK, let's talk," he said.

"Could we take a couple of days off and go somewhere that will give us some time alone? No phones ringing, no staff walking in. No obligations except for each other. I flew all night and landed on your strip. For now, I'm going to your bed for some badly needed sleep. You go do what you must. This afternoon, wake me up, and I'll fly my plane to Nashville. You need to be behind my aircraft. After you wake me up, we'll decide where we want to go. Just think about that today. Tony, I want you as you want me, but not until we decide where we are going for a few days. I'll leave that up to you."

"Very well, but when I return, we'll have a meal before we go," he said.

"The keyword here is CANCEL all others except each other. Got that?"

"Gotcha. Want to go to the beach or mountains?" he asked.

"You decide, but I just want to be alone with the man I've fallen in love with," she said.

"Okay, the mountains of Yellowstone in a cabin if available." He smiled and nodded.

She got up and made her way to bed. He went to his vehicle to settle a few disputes and meet with staff.

She was asleep as soon as her head hit the pillow. He went to work with a big smile on his Italian face.

The police chief was first on his agenda. The report stated: "Many fistfights after the concert." No one was hurt, no big problem. Complaints: not enough motel rooms, most cafés closed, a lot of gas stations closed, and long lines to buy tickets at the concert hall.

Complimentary: Good show. The concert hall building is very nice. The city people are kind and appreciative. Diners and hamburger stands, especially Pal's, are outstanding. The parking scheme using trollies is a great idea. Security is always available and broke up a lot of fights.

Wal-Mart's investigative people described where they wanted their location and were pleased that the mayor had given them a choice. The other area, located near the industrial park, was ideal for building low-income housing, which was needed as soon as possible. He called Pete Oats and told him to start clearing the property at once. Then, he called Samantha to announce to the newspaper the incoming Wal-Mart and the new housing area. He called Casey and asked him to alert all the construction people to prepare themselves to bid on the upcoming housing project.

He asked Casey, "Did you think about a mobile home park, an RV park, and an exclusive double-wide park? Would that be appropriate since bids would be out to construct low-income homes? In thinking about it, what will we need in terms of properties? And what about the original plan of not allowing the city's population to exceed the properties we have now?"

"Well, Tony, we are running out of property, that's for sure, but folks who maintain our services and employees at low-income businesses can't afford much. The majority are living in our apartments, which is driving me crazy with non-payment of rent. I've hired a person to oversee this problem, and we're recovering the rent owed from non-payers. He is on top of the issues there. However, those living in the apartments want their own homes. Therefore, the low-cost homes would be more acceptable," said Casey.

"I see, and I agree. Who is this person overseeing the apartments?" Tony asked.

"Samantha actually did the hiring. His name is Carl Salam. I don't know much about him except that he gets the job done," said Casey.

"I want to meet him sometime," said Tony.

"OK, I'll set it up," said Casey.

"Not for a week, though. Believe it or not, I'm going on a short vacation," said Tony.

Next, he called Samantha and told her, "I'm leaving for a week with Harriet. Hell, Sam, I'll just say it—I'm in love with her, and I want to find a cabin somewhere and get to know her," said Tony.

"Boss, I'm not surprised by how you feel about her. I had Bud run a background check on her, and she is exactly what you need," said Samantha.

"You did what?" he screamed. "Sam, why?"

"We all protect and love you, and we just wanted to know more about her in case you asked," said Samantha.

There was silence for a while until Tony asked, "Well, what did you learn?"

"OK, first of all, she is a retired Marine Lt. Colonel. She works as a pilot now in Nashville. Never married, good credit, has a sister in Pensacola, where both grew up. Her dad was a jet fighter in Korea and the last part of World War II. He was killed in a plane crash. Her mother passed away two years later. She graduated from the Naval Academy and Navy Flight School in Pensacola. Was engaged once, but there's no record of his name. She's a concert pianist who has played in all the big concert venues. Roman Catholic, and at one time, she considered becoming a nun."

"Sam, what if I ask her to marry me?"

She laughed and said, "My heart will be broken because I thought you would ask me."

"You're too young, plus you're in love with someone else," said Tony.

"Well, anyway, boss, have a good vacation. We'll hold down the fort until you return," said Samantha.

"Hey, Boss! Do you need help finding a cabin?" she asked.

"What do you have in mind?" he asked.

"New Hampshire or Quebec," she said.

"Perfect. When can you make the reservations?"

"Call me back in ten minutes," she said.

Fifteen minutes later, he called her back. "Well, where are we going?"he asked.

"New Hampshire. Cabin d' Heaven. Fly into Burlington, then rent a car to South Hero. You may get the keys and directions at the airport. And, Boss, you'd best buy food before you leave the big town. Your cabin is on the lake. Take the weapon in the plane with you," she said.

"Samantha, what weapon?" he asked.

"A rifle and a pistol, plus ammo," she said. "Boss, there's a law enforcement badge with the weapons. If you don't cross over into Canada, our cops will leave you alone. Just tell them Bud set this up for you," she said.

"I'm going to give Bud a raise," he said.

"Hey, what about me? I did all the work!" she said.

"Samantha, I'll give you away when you marry. Isn't that a raise?"

He finished up at his office, then went on "Cowboy Way" to the clothing store and bought himself and Harriet a wardrobe that would be adequate for where they were going. Then, he went home.

He phoned the pilot and gave him the destination and estimated time of departure. He got a call from Patricia, telling him about recent happenings.

"A new guy from Texas just walked into the studio and told Sonny he was looking for a break. He has his own songs to audition. Sonny says he's damn good, and we should sign him and make him an opening act for Roy to start with," she said.

"OK, but clean him up. Send him to a western store to pick out a couple of show outfits and some clothing for around town. Record him now, and if you and Tony are still satisfied, get him an apartment and about $500 for walking-around money. But first, get him a drug test. What's his name?" he asked.

"LaDale Simpkins."

"LaDale Simpkins? What kind of name is that?" Tony laughed.

"OK, Dad, we'll be cautious, but when you return, drop by the studio and listen to this melodious hillbilly's tapes."

"Now, where are you going?" she asked.

"To New Hampshire. We've got a cabin rented there and will stay a week. No phones allowed. When we go for supplies, I'll check in just to let you know how we are. Samantha engineered all of this, so I'm beginning my first vacation," said a happy Tony.

On his way home to Harriet, he stopped at Sol's Jewelry and immediately went to the counter that featured wedding rings. This was outside his knowledge of social graces. He had never bought a ring in his life. Finally, he selected a set and guessed her size. It was $10,000. He never quibbled about the price—he just bought it.

As he entered his home, an aroma entered his soul when he opened the back door. Harriet stood in a new beige slacks outfit, wearing a simple golden necklace, a golden top, and matching beige pumps. Her hair was elegant, and her smile was brilliant.

"Hi, Tony, come on in."

He then broke the news that they were going to New Hampshire and had a cabin. She clapped her hands excitedly and said, "Let's go now!"

Tony grinned from ear to ear and said, "Hope you don't mind, but I took the liberty of buying you some Western clothing. They are in a suitcase in my car. Got you some boots also."

"How did you know my sizes?" she asked.

"Noticed the manufacturing tag's name and told the ladies who work for me, and they did the rest. Just stopped by the Western clothing store, added luggage, and packed up for you. Hope this is okay with you. I know a lot of ladies don't like surprises."

"Well, I do. Remember, I'm a Marine. I know how to adjust to about any situation. Now tell me, how are we going to get to New Hampshire?"

"In my jet, being serviced and fueled as we speak. You can ride in the second chair if you wish," he said.

"Well, I could, but I prefer sitting on your lap," she giggled.

He went into his bedroom, changed clothes, got his toiletries and a couple of bottles of Jack Daniel's bourbon, and took his lady and her luggage to the airport, where his plane was waiting and ready.

That afternoon, they arrived in Burlington, where his newly rented Cadillac sedan was parked. Harriet was accustomed to this type of treatment for some of the people she delivered at airports, but this was a first for her.

After landing, they drove toward South Hero, but first, they went into a huge grocery store and spent an hour buying food, condiments, plates, knives, forks, etc., along with four bottles of wine and a case of beer.

They arrived at the cabin around six-thirty p.m. Tony unloaded, put the wine and beer in the refrigerator, and was walking out the door when he heard her say, "Tony, lock the door and come here." She was in the bedroom with only candles glowing. She stood completely nude near the headboard and said, "I've been waiting for you all my life. Never have I ever fallen in love like this. I want you so much, and whatever you feel for me, I'll find out tonight."

He put his right hand in his leather vest's inside pocket and brought out the rings he'd bought in Cripple Creek.

"You don't deserve to wait anymore." He opened his hand and presented the rings. "Harriet, I know so little about you, but I know this: I love you, and I want you with me for the rest of my life. When you look at me, it is like seeing sunshine rising over a mountain—breathless, just breathless. Will you take this ring and marry me as soon as possible, my precious, breathless lover?"

He slipped a ring onto her left ring finger, and Tony noticed it fit. She took his hand and tugged him to the candlelight, where she ripped the cowboy shirt with pearl buttons open, unbuckled his cowboy rodeo buckle, and unsnapped his jeans. She pushed him down on the bed and removed his boots, socks, pants, and underwear. For the remainder of the night, they made love over and over again. The candlelight cast an aura of extreme love over the loving middle-aged couple.

The next morning, while she slept, Tony took a walk outside to grasp their environment. It was gorgeous, he thought. Plucking a hickory nut pod from a limb dripping toward the ground, he thought of his home in Arkansas. Funny, he thought, the more I try to change my life, the easier it gets. Falling in love with Harriet was the best thing he'd done in a long time. Winning in poker was fairly easy, but nothing like this. Building a city was difficult, but he enjoyed it—though nothing like loving her.

Question though—what do I do next in my life with her? She hasn't mentioned what, if any, change she wants to make or, for that matter, has already made. Do I wait for her to tell me, or do I ask? He walked about twenty more yards and stopped directly in front of the front door, anticipating the answers to many of the questions he'd been asking himself. He opened the big green wooden door and entered.

"Good morning, Tony, my husband, my love. Where have you been?" she said.

"Morning, Harriet. Been walking down a fertile path, thinking about what paths we will make," he said.

"And what did you come up with?" she asked.

"Truthfully, nothing. But I did learn that for the remainder of our lives together, I figure we'll discuss and work out all our problems and gifts," he said.

"Oh, I hope so. I'm tired of having to answer all of life's questions. I need you to help me along the way," she said.

"Then you still want to get married?" he asked.

"Must you ask? Indubitably, I will, Tony!" she said.

He started laughing as he reached for her.

"Wait a moment. Do you want me to tell you how I wish we could wed?" she said.

"Well, that would be a good thing since I have never done a marriage before," he said.

"As simple as possible. I realize you are a powerful man and are accustomed to doing things on a large order, but I'm just a Marine who can fly, and it's my custom to make matters small. What do you think about Vegas?" she said.

"No, a small wedding with our families only—getting married in the church at Cripple Creek," he said.

"Sounds like a plan to me. You wear a tux, though, and I'll pick out a gown. You get a photographer, and we'll have a reception at home. I'm retiring as soon as we get back. Drop me off in Nashville, and I'll move right away. We'll set the date according to when Father Duncan is available. I'll bring my sister with me when I move if that is okay," she asked.

"Yes. Tell me again, what is your sister's name?" he asked.

"It's Margaret, and she is a widow. Works with the stock market there," said Harriet.

"Does she have any children?" he asked.

"A son who's getting his pre-med degree at the University of Alabama-Birmingham and a daughter who's a nurse on the North Dakota Indian reservations. They'll be invited to the wedding, but I'll let Margaret handle that," she said.

"I'll call Father Duncan at once and have him give us three different dates, and after I get them from the schedule, you and I will determine the proper date. I'll have my daughter and grandson there. That's all," he said.

They arrived in Nashville on Saturday afternoon and dropped Harriet off. He had the pleasure of meeting Margaret at the commercial flight building. She was attractive but older than Harriet.

"Oh! Tony, I've been wanting to meet you since Harriet told me about you. Hey! You do look like Dean Martin after all," Margaret said, smiling.

The entire entourage assembled. In the small ring of people were the sisters' friends, who just wanted to shake his hand, look at her ring, and squeal! It seemed all were happy and hovered around the couple until a gunshot exploded, and Tony fell to the ground, wounded. Squeals and laughter now turned into screams and shouts as an escaped bald man ran out the open back door into a black auto and raced away.

Tony was prostrate on the floor. Harriet, weeping uncontrollably, held Tony's head in her lap. Blood was running profusely from his right side.

It seemed an eternity before the ambulance arrived and loaded Tony. Margaret and Harriet followed the wild ambulance, its lights flashing, siren blaring, and horn blasting as they made their way through traffic to Vanderbilt Hospital's emergency room, where a team of medical personnel awaited the arrival of the ambulance. Margaret let Harriet out at the door while she parked.

Nurses worked frantically to keep him alive. On his person were identification and medical information that aided the hospital. However, since he was such an important person, his information card revealed his position as Mayor of Cripple Creek, Arkansas. The clerk phoned Samantha at City Hall and informed her that her boss had been shot with a revolver and was in critical condition. The clerk wanted to speak to his next of kin. After gathering as much information as possible about the shooting, Samantha gave her Patricia's number, then phoned General McCall, as he was President of the City Council, and asked him to report to her office.

Next, she received a call from a screaming Patricia, asking if Samantha could contact the pilot of the jet and have him return to homeport, pick her up, and deliver her back to Nashville. Samantha advised her to calm down; Tony was not dead and was receiving the best care. She then phoned the pilot on his personal phone and advised him to return to Cripple Creek to escort Patricia back to Nashville. He acknowledged and went to work immediately.

Meanwhile, she called Bud, told him what had happened, and instructed him to meet the jet and accompany Patricia back to Nashville. On his way to the airport, Bud phoned the Nashville Police Department to learn what he could about the shooting and the latest updates. He was told they would call him personally as soon as more information was available.

General McCall arrived at City Hall while Samantha was meeting with her assistants. She was informing them of what had happened and how they were expected to respond. Seeing the General, she dismissed them to return to work while she escorted him into the council chambers. To her surprise, the General was very calm and asked appropriate questions. He only requested to be kept updated on any and all developments. He acknowledged that he was now in charge of the city and would remain in the council chambers. He then asked, "Should we contact the rest of the council and have them report to City Hall?"

"Yes, sir, I think that is appropriate," said Samantha.

Immediately, the General phoned the other council members and told them this was an emergency. He instructed them to come to City Hall immediately and to report directly to the council chambers, avoiding discussions with anyone about the call or any potential rumors.

In Nashville, in the surgery room, Tony was undergoing an operation to have a .38 bullet extracted from his appendix area. Many pints of blood had been transfused into his veins, but he was unconscious and unaware of what was happening. Once the staff realized Harriet was engaged to Tony, they informed her of the situation. They also told her that Patricia was on the way and that her plane was landing in Cripple Creek. Harriet phoned Samantha at City Hall and provided an updated version of events. She also told her she would send her sister to the Nashville airport to pick up Patricia.

Harriet then phoned Margaret and asked her to return to the commercial airport to retrieve Patricia and bring her to Vanderbilt Emergency Room.

Samantha entered the council room and informed them of what had happened.

"Ya'll, somebody shot Tony at the commercial airport in Nashville. He is in grave danger. The trauma team is working on him. He is unconscious but alive. He and Harriet were on their way home after getting engaged to marry. He dropped her off, and she was moving here. Some guy, dressed in a dark suit, came out of nowhere, shot him, ran out of an open door, and got into the backseat of a car before driving away. Police are investigating the incident.

I asked Chief Detective Bud to accompany Patricia to Nashville. First, to take care of her. Second, to meet with the Nashville police and gather any information they have on this attempt on Tony's life. Harriet is with Tony near the surgery room, trying to learn his condition.

According to the act ya'll passed, General Ambrose McCall is the acting mayor. Now, I know how much our mayor is loved by the citizens of this town. I suggest ya'll decide how to inform them as quickly as possible, rather than having thousands of people trying to get in here. Once you tell me what to do, we need to shut down this office and hold a press conference. I've already called Sam Bucknell and asked him to open the small concert hall.

Now, remember, we have a press secretary who is on the way to the concert hall and, along with Sam, will be prepared to inform the public. Excuse me a minute, I'm getting a call from Harriet."

"Hello, Miss Harriet, tell me what's happening."

"He is still in surgery. The bullet has been removed, and the bleeding has been stopped. We won't know anything else until the X-rays come back, and the surgery is completed. I'll call you if there are any changes."

"Very well, I will inform the council of your report. Now, Patricia is on the way with Bud. Please have someone pick her up at the commercial aircraft waiting area. Bud will remain at that building with the Nashville police to learn what they have uncovered in their investigation," said Samantha.

"Very well, I'll keep you updated," said Samantha.

She collected General McCall, and they departed City Hall for the concert room. As they got out, the General started toward the podium.

Samantha said, "General, go on, but give me some time alone. I'll join you shortly."

When he resumed walking, she could not control what happened next. Tears and sobs overcame her. Love for her boss and her mentor was more than she could stand. Standing still for a while became shaking at the possibility Tony could die.

Suddenly, a huge hand wrapped around her left shoulder, and a bass voice said, "Miz Samantha, you gotta pull yoself together.

170

Folks are 'pending on you. Git up dere and tell 'um what happened and how he be. You kin do it. Ol' Sam will walk you up dere. Now, les' go."

They started walking toward the stage, and just as soon as she placed her foot on the stage, her phone rang. When she looked down at it, she saw it was Harriet.

"Hello, Miss Harriet, what is the latest?"

She listened as the room murmured, her countenance changing rapidly from worry to a smile.

"Oh, thank you. I'll report what you have told me."

Chapter 24

As you folks know by now, I've only lived here about a year. I'm from St. Louis but lived on post at Fort Leonard Wood in my job as the ranking general of the Corps of Engineers. You know, my job with the Corps began after I graduated from West Point and served first in Korea, then in many areas of the United States.

It was during my time stationed in New Orleans that I heard of a true hero who wasn't involved in combat as we normally think of it. He was designated to go from being stationed in New Orleans to the Red River of Louisiana as the supervisor of the project to clear the river of the "Great Log Raft," a formidable obstruction to navigation. His name was Lieutenant Eugene A. Woodruff, and what occurred was during the year 1873.

In September of that year, Lieutenant Woodruff left his workboats and crew on the Red River to visit Shreveport and recruit a survey party. When he arrived in Shreveport, he found the city in the grip of a yellow fever epidemic. Fearing that he might carry the disease to his workmen if he returned to his camp, he made a decision. Now get this: Woodruff elected to remain in Shreveport and tend to the sick, volunteering his services to an organization named The Howard Association, a Louisiana disaster relief charity. He traveled from house to house in his carriage, delivering food, medicine, and good cheer to the sick and dying. He contracted the disease and died of it in Shreveport on September 30th of that year.

In his eulogy:

"He died because he was too brave to abandon his post even in the face of a fearful pestilence and too humane to let his fellow beings perish without giving all in his power to save them. His name should be cherished, not only by his many personal friends but by the Army, as one who had lived purely, labored faithfully, and died in the path of his duty…His conduct of the great work on which he was engaged at the time of his death will be a model for all similar undertakings, and the completion of the work a monument to his memory."

Guess what? His commanding officer then assigned Eugene's brother, George, the task of completing the work. On November 27th of that year, the engineers broke through the raft, finally clearing the Red River for navigation.

In a way, that is what is happening here. Our leader is in a terrible way but is going to survive, I'm sure. He was one of my "boys" in Vietnam—wounded and decorated while protecting our "Tunnel Rats." Our positions keep changing, but we have a great deal of affection for each other. I am proud to stand in his stead until he returns. I'll appreciate all of you supporting me and, of course, him. I'll continue residing at my wonderful house that he had built for me in Country Club Estates. I will be in this room at my office.

"Bless you, and now let us begin," said the General.

On the second week after surgery, Tony woke up again. He had lost a lot of weight, grown a full beard, and was still not aware of what had happened.

He looked at Harriet and witnessed her compassion and love.

"Hey, gorgeous," he said in a weak voice."Are we married yet?" "Have you been here very long?" "What happened to me?" "Where am I?"

Harriet started laughing and said, "Hold on, stud, give me a break, and I'll answer. First of all, you were shot by a man wearing a black suit and who is bald. He ran out the back door at the commercial terminal here in Nashville, into a black car, and got away. The Nashville Police and your chief detective, Bud Lee, are investigating.

"You have lost a lot of blood and have been here two weeks—probably a little longer. Dr. Cunningham will be here around four o'clock and talk to us about sending you home. No, we are not married yet, but folks here think we are since I've been here so long. Do you have any more questions?"

"Yes, what is your last name?" Tony asked.

"Hudson."

"Oh yeah, now I remember. When are we going to get married?" he asked.

Chapter 25

Prior to Tony's arrival back home, Patricia gained stature in the community by bringing in big musical acts to perform at the Cripple Creek Concert Hall and occasionally at "Tater Graham's." She used many female acts at Tater Graham's because the fans were mostly women and appreciated giving "girls" a chance. Most of the singers had recorded at "famous" studios or dropped by to say hello and ask about available contracts.

One such "girl" was a delightful lass from Wetumpka, Alabama, the birthplace of the legendary Hank Williams Sr. Her name was Donna Gregory. She was around twenty-one and very pretty, but above all, her vocals were so much like the infamous Patsy Cline that it was hard to distinguish her from the beloved Virginia singer. Donna didn't attempt to be an impersonator but honored Patsy in her act. She made a 'crack' in the act by saying she'd rather sound like Patsy than Willie Nelson.

Patricia wanted to use her in a concert appearance along with two other young people who could feature the western swing band sound that Tony wanted to reintroduce to the world.

Tony's grandson, a cadet at the Naval Academy, found out about his grandfather's situation and arranged to catch a flight to Nashville to see Tony. Unfortunately, Tony was in a deep recovery sleep and couldn't be aroused. He did, however, meet Harriet and was very impressed with her. She, too, had graduated from the Academy and had been selected for Marine flight school. They connected, and she made arrangements to fly to Cripple Creek. After a couple of days there with his mother, he'd be flown to Annapolis.

He surprised his mother at the studio, and after she calmed down, she noticed an attractive honey blonde standing there, agape.

"Hi, I'm Anthony Gianni. She's my mother."

At first, she just stood there with her mouth still open. She had never seen a man so handsome. Hell, she thought, he looks like Elvis, only younger.

"I'm Donna. Your mother is giving me some advice on my career."

"What do you do?" he asked.

"I'm a singer, but I'm just starting. There's a possibility of recording and appearing in a concert, I hope."

He then turned back to his mom and said, "Mother, I'm starving to death. Is there someplace here where we could eat?"

"Yes. Bet you'd like to have some southern BBQ, wouldn't you?"

"You bet. Could she go with us?" he asked.

"Sure, but I get to 'hog' the conversation," said Patricia.

"Okay. Is that all right with you, Donna?" asked Anthony.

"Now, Tony, there is someone else you must meet, but he is busy at City Hall directing some visitors to a house he's building. His name is Roman, and he is my husband," she said.

"YOUR HUSBAND? You mean I now have a dad?"

"Yep. How long can you stay here?" she asked.

"Another day, and I must meet him," stated Anthony.

The three loaded up in Patricia's car and drove to Memphis BBQ Café. Anthony and Patricia held an old-fashioned Italian get-together. A girl from Alabama had never enjoyed herself so much, and this glorious-looking man did not desert her at all. They "accidentally-on-purpose" continually touched each other.

Donna only asked, "When will you be discharged?"

His answer was, "I will make the Navy or Marines my lifetime job."

Her second question was, "What is your major?"

"Aerodynamics," he said, looking directly into her blue-green eyes.

They returned to the studio for a short period, then Patricia and Anthony went to her home, and Donna to her motel room. She had to prepare for her show at Tater Graham's bar that night. Anthony said he'd be there if he could find civilian clothes to wear rather than the Navy whites.

While he took a much-needed nap, his mother went to the western clothing shop on 'Cowboy Way' and bought him what he needed. The shirt was red, like the one she thought Elvis wore in one of his movies.

Donna rested, then prepared her voice for that night's show. She knew the song plan, and in the act, she normally danced and sang to a member of her audience. It was a big crowd-pleaser. She knew exactly who she would dance with—Anthony, the grandson of a very powerful man.

That evening, before she left to do her gig, she closed her eyes and dreamed of being Anthony's wife. Whatever the future would be, tonight was her opportunity to impress the only man she'd met since becoming an adult who truly "turned her on." He was the man she wanted to marry, but both of them wanted two different worlds. How could she get him?

Her mother's voice, from the day she was a teen cheerleader, echoed in her soul: "Just be yourself, but if you are in love with him, don't let him go." She started smiling then, and it froze on her beautiful face—because Anthony noticed it the minute she came on stage.

She opened with Fats Domino's version of "Four Winds," then flowed into Carl Perkins' song "Honey Don't." After a small monologue, she moved into the two "Blue Moons" Elvis had done. The place was rocking and yelling for more. She did another monologue, but this time about Patsy Cline.

The opening chords of "Crazy" began, and she stepped off stage, strolled to the table where Anthony, Patricia, and another guy sat, took Anthony's hand, and pulled him up to her. Wrapping her arms around him, she began singing "Crazy" exactly as Patsy had sung it.

The female population in that dance hall stopped dancing and surrounded them. Anthony never took his eyes off hers. The satin burnt-orange outfit clung to her wonderful body as if she had been poured into it. They danced provocatively, but not as if they were making love. It appeared as it should—this could be the start of a great romance.

Upon completion, Anthony said, "I didn't really know how to dance, but I couldn't say no. Donna, thank you for allowing me to be a part of your act. I shall never forget it."

He sat back down and looked all around. People were still standing still but now had a longneck beer in their hands. Two very young girls came over after Donna went back on stage and sang *I Fall to Pieces* and asked him to dance. He smilingly declined but bought both a beer.

Patricia was in some type of never-never land and began looking at Anthony with different eyes. Her son was now an adult, and people reacted to him strangely. Women saw him as someone to conquer and take home. This girl had fallen in love with him, she suspected. Nevertheless, tomorrow he would catch a flight back to Pensacola, where he was temporarily studying to be a pilot. In two more weeks, he'd go back to Annapolis for one more year of studies, and then she would see him graduate. She hoped her dad could accompany Roman and her to see the services.

Her plans for Donna were to place her as an opening act for the New Christy Minstrels, whom she had just signed. They had a lead singer with a very unusual voice that could be a big thing one day. His name was Ken Rogers.

The next morning at breakfast, the conversation got more serious since it centered around Granddaddy Gianni.

"What happened, Mom?" he asked.

"You grew up in Little Italy; you know the people there. Well, one of them hired a hitman to kill your Granddaddy."

"Why? He hasn't lived there in a long time," Anthony said.

"He got MiMi pregnant with me, but his dad, Anthony Senior, didn't believe he was the true father and sent him away. Only the family knew this, but the Mafia saw it differently, and someone swore vengeance on Tony. They went after him in Biloxi, but he escaped. They killed his girlfriend instead, but that wasn't good enough. They were going to kill you and me, but since you had joined the Navy, they left you alone. In addition, since your Granddad brought us both here for protection, they decided to make another move and shoot him. Surprises me they got him in Nashville. Don't know how the shooter learned where he would be."

Tony had promised Donna he'd get in touch with her today, but he was leaving, and he wanted to look around this place. Why not do both? He phoned her and told her to be prepared. His mom and Roman wanted to take him out to the country club for dinner.

After he showered and shaved, Roman came by and picked him up. Then, from the Cripple Creek Hotel downtown, they began their journey. First, they went downtown, where they were shown the statue of his granddaddy. They passed through downtown, past the mayor's house, northward up Market Road for two miles to the concert hall, then east to the rodeo arena, then up the winding road climbing the mountain. Mayor Gianni didn't know that the Department of the Interior had answered the request to name the mountain Mount Reagan because a mountain near the former president had been selected for that name. He didn't know what he'd want to rename it.

They took zip line rides down and back up, and Donna loved it. Then they went east on the big highway to the industrial park and then to the south side to the country club area.

At last, Roman dropped them off at the hotel, and he proceeded to a job site near Huntsville.

They simply went into her room and completed what both had been yearning for.

Roman finished work, went by the hotel again, and picked up Anthony for dinner that night with his mother. Both men had big smiles on their masculine faces. Anthony thought hard about him and told himself, I will like this guy.

Chapter 26

A suite had been set up in the area near the lobby at Vanderbilt Hospital, giving Harriet a place to be more comfortable and more room for the nurses and technicians to do their jobs more adequately. Tony and Harriet were sitting there, having their coffee and reading the newspapers when she finally asked, "Honey, I know we must be more careful in the future, but how are we to do that with your positions in life?"

Silence followed for a while, then Tony answered, "Unless the one person who shot me reappears, I, or rather we, must go into hiding for the remaining days God has given us. I really want us to go about our life in Cripple Creek. I love being the mayor of my city. Now, you too must go until the shooter is caught. The person who shot me will not fail to continue trying to eradicate me."

"How do you know this?" Harriet asked.

"I spoke with Zero Zandt. He tells me the money set aside to kill me is now gone. The person trying to hit me is kin to the capo who first started this. His insurance money has been paying for a long time, and if the culprit after me isn't successful soon, he'll run out of money and probably do something stupid. He'll not have any more budget money to complete his task and will give or lay his life on the line in his attempt."

"Why has this been an ongoing mission?"

"My dad was too powerful for an inter-family war, so Annett's father decided to get me. That would bring about satisfaction. Trouble was, I was in Vietnam, and they figured I'd be killed there. All would be peaceful until I crossed the commanding general of the air base in Biloxi by screwing his wife. It was he who arranged to meet with her dad in New York. Rumor is the general contributed funds to have me wiped out. I was not vulnerable enough in Biloxi for him to do the job himself. His wife convinced him to take her away from so much temptation, and she was sent home to some place in Virginia. I understand she killed herself from an overdose of something. Zero told me all of this and assured me that the majority of the Mafia wants this problem to be hushed up. The rest of them don't care."

"Tony, are you saying if the guy who shot you gets caught or killed, this all would end?"

"Yes, it looks that way."

"What if he never tries again or is caught without your knowledge and you are in hiding? Could or would you reappear?"

"No! Until the shooter is identified and captured or it is proven he is dead, I will have to be incognito for the rest of my life."

"You keep talking in the singular and not in the plural. What about me?"

"Why should you have your life so sardonically existing day to day? 'Hitters' would need to shoot you also, but most would rather rape you."

"Harriet, you couldn't live the life I'd have to put you in. No permanent place or time. Remember that show on TV called *The Fugitive*?"

"Yes, but you think it would be that extreme?"

"I do, and even worse."

"Where would we go?"

"West, maybe northwest. I'd need to change my appearance drastically in order to make money."

"I don't understand. Why would that be necessary?"

"I can't show as if I have a lot of cash and can't withdraw from existing funds. That would give me away. I would have to do what

I do best—play poker in non-casino places. Win just enough to move on and live another week or so."

"You've thought this out, haven't you?"

"All except for one thing—what about you?"

"Meaning?"

"Can I live without you, not will I live without you?" he asked.

"Would or will you, if I understand the question?" she said.

"My answer is no, I can't. I can take money out, and we will go to Europe to live. I speak Italian as well as Spanish, so we could hide out somewhere over there," he said.

"Well, smartass, I speak French and German," she said, smiling.

"Next statement I will make is: will you still want to marry me?"

"What a proposal! When? How?"

"Call Father Duncan and have him make all arrangements. Remember, just family. The next day after the wedding, we'll leave on a 'honeymoon.' Trouble is, for family, we can't tell them we won't return."

She looked so sad instead of happybut obeyed the man she loved so much and constantly worried about. Father Duncan and she settled on three days from now. The priest was ecstatic about this wedding. He liked them both, and since they were born Roman Catholics, he felt their marriage would be a good one.

Next, she phoned Patricia and asked her to purchase the cake and have it delivered to the dining area of the country club. She then called the concierge at the club and asked him to arrange the reception for eighteen people. Piped-in music would be acceptable. Colors: blue, pink, and white. She asked him to order her a dress and

Tony a navy blue tux. Tony was going to phone the general and ask him to be his best man. He also asked the general to get his marriage license in Huntsville. The judge there was a friend and would comply with this unusual request. Harriet's birth records would be faxed in, as well as Tony's. The general was also asked to have "Sam" pull up his and fax them.

Harriet was in another room talking to Margaret and asked her to come with them on this trip and stay for the wedding. She needed her in many ways. Her escort would be General McCall.

A photographer would be worked in with the country club, and instead of Tony's house, the dining room would be acceptable. The concierge's name was Antoine, and Harriet phoned him to give all sizes of the bride and groom, including shoe sizes.

Tony's doctor arrived that afternoon and announced he could return home but insisted that his appointment at Vanderbilt be met in ten days. Tony told him that would be impossible. Doctor Mac asked the reason for that. Tony just responded that it had to do with his being shot in the first place. Doctor Mac hated to do this, but he'd have to announce he would discontinue treating him. Tony asked him if, in case of a change, he could call him if that would be permissible. Reluctantly, the doctor agreed. "What is with that man? He nearly died, but we saved him," he told his assistant.

They loaded up and went to the commercial airstrip, the place where he'd been shot, and had to wait for a while with Bud guarding him. LaDale and Margaret waited outside in an ambulance with the attendants. They would load him up when his jet arrived first and then the passengers. Harriet would not fly second seat on this but instead assist with the glucose bottle.

The sun was shining for a November day. Clouds were approaching from the west, but Harriet overheard the weather forecast, and it appeared to be pleasant.

Tony's jet arrived on time and taxied up to the loading area. At the same time, the fuel truck pulled up to place the nozzle in the fuel tank and top off the tanks. It didn't take long to do this, and shortly after, the ambulance reloaded Tony and Bud, pulled up to the ramp, and began the task of positioning the gurney properly. Some seats had been removed before they left Cripple Creek, creating a vacant space for Tony's gurney. Adequate seats for passengers were still available.

Within an hour, they were flying over Nashville, headed for the northwest area of Arkansas.

Chapter 27

"Why?"

"Damn it, Aunt Louise, just look in my mother's phone book and give me the phone number of Zero Zandt. I'll hold," said a stressed-out Tony.

"It's (643) 877-2012. And that's all I have," said the aunt with anger.

"Thanks, Aunt Louise. Are you okay?"

"No money to go to the doctor."

"I'll have my assistant phone you and find out how much you'll need tomorrow."

"Great, Tony. You have always been my favorite."

"And you too, Aunt Louise."

His doctor entered with a smile on his beefy face and said, "Mr. Gianni, Miss Hudson said you want to load up on a plane and go home to Arkansas. Is that true?"

"Only if you know I'll be correct in doing this."

"Good answer. Yes, our records reveal you are a strong man and are healing nicely. Once home, you still need to take it easy. No stressful situations. Wait another month before you go back to work."

"Thank you, Doc. Let's get things going, hon!"

She phoned the pilot and gave him an ETA to load up. Then she phoned Bud and told him to get security from the police department to escort him to the aircraft. The weather was dubious, but an attempt could be made.

"What did you say, Bud?"

"You're going back with us, aren't you?"

"Ma'am, one of Famous Studio's rising stars needs a ride back to Cripple Creek. Would that be okay?"

"What's his name?" she asked coolly.

"Never heard of him. Let me ask Tony."

She asked if LaDale Simpkins could ride back with them. "He works at Famous."

"Yes, but only if he agrees to change his name," answered Tony.

She laughed and told Bud what Tony said. He would be riding with Bud, so everything should be all right. The kid actually wasn't a kid, just a man of around thirty who dressed like the "cowboys" that hung out around bars near the Ryman. A strange thing about him struck Tony's searching eyes—his long hair was actually a wig. But Tony, being a gentleman, decided not to mention this faux pas.

Anyway, they loaded Tony up along with Harriet, Bud, and LaDale on a pleasant day and flew to the wonderful city of Cripple Creek, Arkansas. Tony was settled in, Harriet rode second chair, and Bud crashed at once. LaDale took his guitar out of the beat-up case and started tuning it.

"Son, haven't heard you do anything. Sonny and Patricia are high on your talent, so, while we are traveling, how about doing some songs?" asked Tony.

"Sure, what do you want?" he asked.

"Oh, why not do some southern gospel to start with, then do a Marty Robbins song, and finish up with some blues?" smiled Tony.

LaDale sat there awhile, just staring at the older man, then began to strum and hum. Surprisingly, he sang:

"I am weak, but Thou art strong,

Jesus, keep me from all wrong,

I'll be satisfied as long

As I walk, let me walk close to Thee.

Grant it, Jesus, hear my plea.

Daily walking close to Thee,

Let it be, dear Lord, let it be."

He stopped for a minute, and a mischievous smile came across his face as he began singing a little differently—same tune but my version of this:

"Just a bowl of butterbeans,

Don't want no collard greens,

Just give me a bowl of butterbeans…"

Tony roared with laughter. LaDale smiled again, very devilishly.

He then finished up with his version of Marty Robbins' *Don't Worry About Me* and a funny blues tune that went:

"There was a dominical rooster and a Shanghai hen,

Run around together, but they ain't no kin,"

And finished:

"If you're ever down South,

Just drop around

To my one-room shanty

On the edge of town.

Oh, sweet woman, treetop tall,

Won't you kindly turn your damper down?"

LaDale smiled and then said, "Whatcha think, boss? Can I make it on stage?"

"Yes, son, believe you got possibilities."

Cripple Creek came up on the horizon as Tony peeked out for only a few minutes, but that was enough to give him his wonderful ecstasy over the town he gave life to.

Harriet was busy aiding the pilot to land and taxi to the terminal. LaDale thanked Tony for "the ride" and said goodbye as the ramp was loaded to the open door for exiting.

A welcome party of around a thousand people surrounded the plane. Singing, shouting, and cheering for their hero could be heard downtown. The ambulance loaded him. They got settled in by greeting the house full of people but excused them shortly as fatigue overtook him. Harriet helped put him in bed, and after he was tucked in, the people bid farewell and orderly left, understanding his condition and expressing how they felt about him.

Once they were alone, Tony beckoned her to sit with him in his suite.

"Honey, there is something you must abide by from now on. No more crowds. No more people just dropping by. I would like to see the General later, but here is something I dread to speak to you about.

Harriet, now I'm sure I am a marked man. Whoever shot me will return to finish the job. In addition, they will murder you also! From this moment on, you must be packing and alert until we leave. Yes, I said leave. Marrying me will be an extreme hardship for you, and I'll seek someone from the F.B.I. to assist me in finding a place that is safe and secure.

We cannot return here. Name changes, social settings changed, appearances changed. Finances abbreviated. No connection to family members for their safety and assurance. We must hide for the remainder of our lives. It will be as if we are dead," he said, sitting up.

She started sobbing and put her arms around him.

"Harriet, it would be best we not get married. You are to leave me and go about your life as it was before. Deny me. Tell people we 'broke up.' But you'll still be in danger and must be careful at all times."

She was shaking her head and screeching, "No! Hell no! I'll never leave you. Don't you know how much I love you? I'm a marked person also. The killer will eventually go after me too," she moaned.

"Tony, is there no way we can handle this better? Get tighter security, get on your cruise ship, and anchor down somewhere? Have the government help us?" she said.

"Honey, is that all?" she asked.

"The only thing else—he exposes himself, and we eliminate him," he said.

"I'm naïve, but couldn't he have given up trying by now?" she asked.

"No, Harriet, the price on my head is probably near a million dollars," Tony remarked. "They don't give up with that much money at stake."

They enjoyed the remainder of the day reading the mail and get-well cards and finally having a good home-cooked meal. Tony told her that since he had lived in the South so long, he was a true "Johnny Reb" now when it came to food. He especially loved sweet iced tea, banana pudding, and black-eyed peas. He was well known as a lover of grilled barbecue. He was looking forward to catching up with his meals.

That night, Tony drifted off with the help of a potent sleeping pill, but around midnight, he heard the sound of a whirring vehicle. He couldn't wake up enough to determine what was happening and fell back to sleep. Later, he was awakened by the sound of a gunshot near him. He came to, hearing the screams of a woman but drifted back, hearing her say his name. Finally, someone lifted his head from the pillow and inserted something in his mouth, then splashed water on his face.

Reality suddenly appeared, and he alertly opened his eyes to see Harriet standing over him, calling his name.

"Tony, I shot him. It was that singer. Wake up, honey, I need you to hold me. I've called the police. Get up, please."

He sat up and saw Harriet in a mess—blood over his bed, a dead body on the floor near where he had been sleeping. Harriet stood in a gown and robe, with blood and some matter on her front, a .357 in her hand.

He stood up, walked over to her, took the weapon, and placed it on the table. Then he put his arms around her and led her out of the room to the kitchen, where he sat her in his chair. He went to the back door and opened it wide for the police he heard approaching. Tony noticed a golf cart parked in his area.

Strange, he thought. I didn't know I owned a golf cart.

He went back to Harriet, who was now very silent, staring straight ahead. Tony gently asked, "What happened?"

Before she could answer, the police arrived. Tony motioned for them to just listen. Again, he asked, "What happened, Harriet?"

Softly, she said, "Heard a noise outside, like a whirling. Got up to check on you but saw a shadow, so I picked up your gun as I came into your room and saw this man with a gun in his hand, pulling the covers back. Don't know what I said, but he turned, and I recognized him. I'm unsure, but I know he aimed his gun toward me and said—

I think—'I'll just get you too.' Then I squeezed my trigger, and he went down. It was LaDale. The same guy that Tony was trying to help. Don't remember much except I fell on LaDale, trying to get to you, and started trying to wake you up. Somewhere, sometime, I remember I had my cell phone in my robe pocket and dialed 911. I was screaming so much from the terror it brought."

The room suddenly filled with men. Tony was removed to another bedroom, and Harriet went to her room to change clothes. Tony called Patricia and asked her to come to his house to be with Harriet. He was surrounded by armed policemen and agents.

Some time later, General Ambrose appeared.

"Glad you're back home. Tony, listen to me closely—it's over. The people who want to kill you are either arrested or, in this case, dead. You and Harriet are safe. You are now with family and friends. The F.B.I. made many arrests yesterday, including a man named Zero something or other. Just get well. We'll help you take care of Harriet."

Two months later, they were married, and Tony resumed his position as mayor. He held that position until he died at the age of 89.Epilogue

A month after Tony arrived home from the hospital in Nashville, a "bull session" that included steaks, etc., was conducted at Tony's pier house for an enlightenment session. Only his closest and most trusted friends were invited to finally learn of the fabled poker game that he attended on an ocean liner many years ago. His invitation included: Casey, Bill, Roy, General, Samantha, Elizabeth, and Father Duncan.

Many steaks and bourbon were consumed just before Tony began:

"I was heavily involved in small-time poker playing in Biloxi. Down there, the entire Dixie Mafia owed me money for gambling debts. Really, all I got from them was notoriety. Went out to Las Vegas and won a lot there. This too gave me more notoriety among the big games in America, which included Chicago and New York. A friend of mine from South Africa, who I think is the richest man in the world, told me of a great opportunity. However, it could cost me a lot of money. A poker game that included the top and richest poker players in the world, and by invitation only. No 'side-men, bodyguards, politicians, or gangsters' would be allowed. Had to bring five million dollars with me and buy chips upon arrival. The game would be played in the ballroom of an ocean liner owned by my friend. Last man standing would be protected and exited with protection. This way the winner would come in as a millionaire and leave as a billionaire. I took a week off and went to New Orleans and sailed with tables filled with well-known millionaires and a few billionaires. All had to wear tuxedos, had suites, and anything to eat, but very little drinking of alcohol. If someone got tipsy, he was escorted to his room and the next boat going ashore would include the 'drunk.'

I started losing at first and began to panic, but one hand of a 'full house' started bringing me back and up. For two days I went back and forth until I drew another full house. The rules never changed. Straight poker or draw poker or a new game named 'Texas Hold 'em.' You knew where you stood all the time. Get broke and out you go. Nothing but winners allowed to stay.

It broke down to two of us. My friend from South Africa and me. I figured he'd try to buy me out, but he was a 'gamer' and wished to win taking all my money.

At this point I was already a billionaire, but just winning was my goal, and I did. Lady Luck was on my side and my moxie stood tall as I made unknown bets.

When I won his ocean liner, we took a break and he went to his room for some sleep. I took a shower, shaved, and changed clothing.

Had a terrific breakfast and went back to the table and waited on him. Didn't count my money but realized I had more money than I had ever accumulated. I placed my five million I'd come in with in trust with the 'house.'

He finally entered but looked terrible. The nap did nothing. It seemed to hurt him. Sitting down, he reached in his pocket for proof of the diamonds, gold, and silver that covered the entire bottom deck of the ship that I now owned, and using a booming voice that tried to intimidate me, he stated, "Sir, you have nearly whipped my ass but it isn't over yet. I propose one hand of straight poker for all you have versus all I have aboard this ship, which I feel I shall win back."

"Accepted," I announced, and you could hear a solid gasp among the players that had previously been beaten by him or me. This was an anthem that silence followed in triumph. I never felt so much confidence.

GAME

First card dealt to me from the new deck was an ace. We just waited. The stakes were established. Next card for me was an 8 of diamonds. He just glared at me and said, "You can back out now and keep the five million you came in with." I shook my head no! Next card dealt was another 8 of clubs; this had just given me a pair, a possibility of a winning hand. He began to pale and this time said nothing. My mouth was dry, so I took a sip of the orange juice I had brought in with me. This wait was the longest yet, but I kept my eyes on him and noticed a tic edging from his left ear—or was it a wiggle? This man is in a strange battlefield, or was it me and my imagination? HE HAS A LOSING HAND AND NOW I'M THE WINNER.

My next card was 8 of diamonds. Yes, dammit, I'm going to win with triple eights. Now it was hard to refrain from a big smile.

The dealer took the remaining cards from the deck and reshuffled and dealt from the bottom. It just laid in power. My hand shook so much I couldn't pick it up, but I knew I had to turn it over. When I did, my heart nearly stopped. Four eights and an ace of spades. I turned them over as he did, and to my astonishment, it was another 8.

I looked up at his brown eyes and saw pure unbelief. Now it was his opportunity to win or lose. He had an ace of diamonds, two deuces, a six of spades, and a three of hearts. I won!! The crowd went wild! My back was sore later from new friends pounding my back.

My opponent grasped my arm and shook my hand. He leaned over and whispered in my ear, "Tony, follow me to my suite and we'll settle up." He then went to the Captain of the ship and spoke to him, and quickly walked away with me following.

In the suite, the first item he gave me was documents declaring me as owner of all metals (gold and silver) on the fifth deck and all diamonds in the safe on the fourth floor. Outside the door was a squad of men that now worked for me and would carry out all his orders. My opponent had trusted them and in his language told them where we all stood. In unison, they murmured they would and went to the elevators as guards of my winnings. The Captain, who carried out the restrictions of the game, approached me and gave me assurance my money would be protected, plus he gave me the deed to the ship.

The Captain directed the crew to port in New Orleans and guard all my possessions, exit the visitors including the former owner of the vessel.

Next, we sat down and I was asked who, what, when, and how I was to dispense my winnings, my personal funds that I brought aboard, and this ship.

I had a bank account in New Orleans, so I phoned the Bank President and invited him aboard when we docked at a designated port. He confirmed after asking me a lot of questions and, in his excitement, mentioned he had a secret place for the metals.

That evening, when we arrived, Mr. David Weatherby, the Bank President, and Mr. Chipper Watkins, Bank Manager, came aboard and for the majority of the night handled my business. To my chagrin, they had bought an empty K-Mart building in Starkville, Mississippi that could house the winnings except for the diamonds, thereby digging a hole, placing iron flooring, sides, and roof that made a capsule hiding the treasure. In addition, it would be guarded as long as I wanted it to be. As you probably know by now, the metals are re-buried in Mountain Ozark and extremely protected. Use the same procedures as our government does when they want something secured. My loans, personally, and for the city if we need, use my winnings as collateral. I have paid taxes on this in years past along with stock and bond ownership.

Our city is in good shape financially. Most of the loans I have made for the city are paid. We collect taxes in the millions now, and our future looks bright. Our employees are our strength. Management couldn't be brighter. Control of city-owned entities is unlike most cities this size. Notice what we began with, that included fly fishing, has given us a very pleasant lifestyle. All of this because of a poker game in the middle of the Gulf of Mexico.

Bill West asked, "Tony, when you came here you moved your winnings from Mississippi to this area. Why?"

Tony answered with a big smile, "Well Bill, it didn't take me long to learn, understand, and trust my new friends up here, including you, the Governor, those that wanted more in their village, and the grace that God had spread out here in my name.

It all accumulated with all of you and the big addition of my natural family and of course, Harriet. Man, have I been blessed. When I was shot by that strange man, I got out of my Strange

Battlefield and all of your souls, as well as our citizens' souls, merged with me.

Bible says—I've read in 1 Peter 3:8, if I remember correctly—"Finally, all of you, be like-minded, be sympathetic, love one another, be compassionate and humble." This is the solution to all of our quests. I love each of you and shall as long as I live. After me, I hope and pray that my grandson, upon completion of his services, takes over many of my business dealings; my daughter enhances the music business here, and I get to enjoy more grandchildren and great-grandchildren. Roy, thanks for what you've done for us in this music endeavor. General, thank you for your input and interest in our city. Doc Sanders, you are such a surprise for me. As a councilman, you stood up and stood tall when I was shot. Bill, you will always be known as a city and business builder for this city. Samantha, my right-hand, my treasure—more important to me than anything buried in the mountain. Father Duncan, who solely built a cathedral in this small town. You, who has prayed over so many, including me, thank you—my friend, my priest. And to Casey, I lift my glass, toasting the person that asked, pushed, trusted, and gave me joy. I thank you, sir, and it is my desire your son will become our next Governor.

Now you know my real story. I'm sure you ask yourself, how could one man be so lucky—or is it blessings, or is it kismet? If I've done any of y'all wrong or insulted you in any way, I apologize.

Now, will you continue working with me in our desire of building a world-class hospital, maybe a university, some type of tourist mecca, or just continuing on with what we have? God bless all of you anyway.

www.ingramcontent.com/pod-product-compliance
Lightning Source LLC
LaVergne TN
LVHW051035070526
838201LV00009B/213